Escape for Chris

by

Ruth Saberton

Copyright

Also by Ruth Saberton

Writing as Jessica Fox

The One That Got Away

Eastern Promise

Hard to Get

Unlucky in Love

Always the Bride

Writing as Holly Cavendish

Looking for Fireworks

Writing as Georgie Carter

The Perfect Christmas

Chapter 1

"And that's to be the last book! We haven't any more in stock I'm afraid, folks. We've totally sold out!"

The manager of the Truro branch of BookWorld had an expression on his face that hovered somewhere between absolute joy and total disbelief. Only two hours earlier, fuelled by a caramel macchiato and aided by two of his keener Saturday staff, he'd lugged one hundred and fifty hardback books down from the stockroom and to the front of the store, where they'd been piled hopefully on a table placed slap in line with the doorway. Ordering such a large amount of expensive hardback copies in these uneasy days of eBooks and Amazon domination was something of a gamble, but he'd had a hunch about this one and his hunches tended to be worth trusting. At half past eleven on this sunny winter's morning the manager was very happy indeed that he'd had faith in this one.

Today's book signing was a huge success by any standards, even for a Saturday in the run-up to Christmas. Such days were always busy, with the pretty cathedral town packed with happy Christmas shoppers, the car parks full by ten a.m. and an air of anticipation keeping the Cornish cold at bay. On Lemon Quay a mini Christmas market did a roaring trade. The coffee shops were crammed with shoppers enjoying gingerbread lattes and mince pies while they got the circulation back into their fingers after lugging carrier bags all around the town; meanwhile, the traditional horse bus, complete with coachman in full Victorian garb, was giving its passengers a leisurely tour of the main streets. Strains of carols drifted on the cold air as the cathedral choir rehearsed for the big day, valiantly competing with the usual Christmas anthems emanating from the shops. Outside the bookstore the pavements were three deep in pedestrians, all wrapped fatly in their winter coats and scarves, and determined to shop until the daylight started to fade and the sun slipped behind the cathedral's spire.

Yes, the book trade was always good on a brisk December Saturday, what with people browsing the shelves for a novel or Jamie Oliver's latest offering – but this morning's activity had been something else entirely. From the minute the cathedral clock had chimed nine and the doors had been unlocked, the store had been rammed. Under normal circumstances, authors sat at their tables, pens clutched in trembling hands and adrift on the sea of carpet while shoppers took the longest route around the shop to avoid making eye contact. When customers did find themselves near the book-signing desk, they generally felt obliged to talk and to buy a novel they'd never really wanted in the first place. Sometimes a savvy author – one who'd read up on marketing or whose agent was switched on – would bring sweets or postcards to tempt the shy book shoppers with goodies. Even so, the queue was never more than a few interested folk or some family and friends recruited to create a buzz. Today, though, it was a very different story. The queue for the signing had even snaked outside into the street, the customers seeming more than happy to stand in the frosty air, hands wrapped around hot drinks from the bookstore's coffee shop, and wait their turn. Inside, the tills were ringing as joyously as the cathedral bells and the entire bookshop was bustling with excitement. As the last customer made her way to the cashier, thrilled with the signed book in her hands, the manager only wished that he'd ordered twice as many.

I should have listened to my daughter, the manager thought ruefully as he apologised to all the disappointed people who'd been unable to buy a signed copy. Sixteen-year-old girls tended to have their fingers on the pulse of the zeitgeist, and this was certainly true of his daughter: when Melanie had heard that Angel and Gemma from *Bread and Butlers* were signing the show's Christmas cookbook in his store, she'd almost popped. He'd been amazed she'd heard of them; One Direction was generally more his daughter's thing than cooking. "Come on, Dad, get with the programme," she'd teased, rolling her eyes. This wasn't a lame cooking show! *Bread and Butlers* was a reality show and everybody watched it. It was the best thing on the telly; Cal was hot, Laurence was even hotter and Angel had the best clothes ever! The bookshop manager had listened in a rather bemused fashion. These days it was almost as though his daughter communicated in a foreign language. Mel's speech was peppered with gangsta slang and text talk: it was all *LOL* this and *lush* the other – as well as his personal worst, *CBA*, which was usually used in reference to homework. Still, once his ears had tuned in to teen speak, he'd managed to gather a few facts and felt even older than his forty-eight years.

These sparkly red and green books that he'd ordered in for the Christmas run-up – which were glossy, satisfyingly fat to hold and crammed full of pictures of glamorous people – accompanied a TV show called *Bread and Butlers*, which apparently was huge. While he'd listened to his eager daughter, the manager had realised that he'd fallen into the popular-culture void between *Newsnight* and *Big Brother*. A quick trip to Google soon revealed this show to be a brilliant cross between *Downton Abbey* and *The Only Way is Essex*, featuring a group of people working together to save a crumbling stately home in Devon. From what he could gather it was a curious mixture of aristocrats, footballers, models and hunky young builders who spent a very unnecessary amount of time walking around with their shirts off like lost members of the Chippendales. There was romance, drama, cooking, posh totty, rows, an ex-Premier League footballer (of whom even a bookish chap like himself had heard), a lively Irish family and even a glamour model or two thrown into the mix. It appeared that the British telly-viewing public simply couldn't get enough of it. The manager had Sky-Plussed a couple of episodes himself; within ten minutes the clever narrative hooks had reeled him in like a square-eyed fish. By the time the final credits had rolled he'd been desperate to find out if Viscount Laurence really had hidden the family diamonds from the bank manager, and whether his eccentric mother was having a fling with a toy-boy builder.

Now he smiled to himself. No wonder today's book signing had been such a success. Mel was right: he did need to "get with the programme"! Everyone wanted a piece of these reality stars, especially since one of them was a bona fide Cornish maid from Bodmin. The Cornish loved their own – and the author of the book, with her cheerful freckled face, ample curves and warm West Country accent, was undoubtedly one of them. He made a mental note to order another big delivery and play this angle up for all it was worth…

Gemma Pengelley, she of the freckled face and curves that were just about kept under control if she ignored all the creamy lattes and slices of thickly iced Christmas cake, put down her pen and flexed her fingers. Ouch. They were really cramped. She guessed this was unsurprising, seeing as she hadn't stopped writing messages and signing her name for over two hours. When Gemma closed her eyes briefly, her scrawling signature was imposed on her retinas. Her brain was hurting from trying to come up with endless original messages. She wished she'd had longer to chat to all the people who'd taken the time to trek into Truro and see her. In Cornwall this was often easier said than done, given that public transport was erratic. Although buses were rumoured to run from some of the outlying villages, in reality they were spotted less than the mythical Morgawr, the county's very own sea serpent.

As she wiggled her aching fingers and tried hard to ignore the smell of cinnamon buns that was drifting down from the first-floor coffee shop, Gemma couldn't help thinking that life was very weird indeed. Here she was sitting at a table with a giant cardboard cut-out of herself on one side (couldn't they have Photoshopped it a bit thinner?) and a viscountess on the other, and signing a cookery book that contained her own favourite recipes. This whole experience had felt even more dreamlike when her old English teacher had shuffled forward in the queue to have his copy signed. Apart from the fact that Gemma had fancied Mr Fuller like crazy when she was fifteen (and even as a twenty-nine-year-old still turned redder than Santa's hat when she spoke to him), she felt a total fraud signing a book for somebody who knew she couldn't spell and wouldn't recognise a complex sentence if one bit her on the bum.

But, then again, life for Gemma Pengelley had taken on a rather unreal quality lately, and she wasn't always certain that she liked this feeling…

"Come on, Gem! Wake up! We're done!" Her best friend and new addition to the aristocracy, Angel Elliott (otherwise known as Lady Kenniston), nudged her with a bony elbow. Her big blue eyes bright with excitement, Angel added: "Now the real fun begins! Let's go shopping!"

"Angel! Ssh!" Gemma glanced around the shop, mortified in case her friend's tactless comment had been overheard by somebody who had just given up an entire Saturday morning to meet them, but the crowds were thinning now that it was lunchtime. The shoppers were all making their way to the smart little bistros and cafés that had sprung up in Truro over the past few years. The city had certainly changed a bit since Gemma and her school pals had spent many happy Saturdays rummaging through the bargain bin in Tammy Girl and eking out a Whopper in Burger King. Now it was all White Stuff and trendy Seasalt clothing, and skinny fries with moules at a chic pavement café on Lemon Quay for lunch – diners cheating the Cornish winter by basking beneath a patio heater.

At the thought of food Gemma's stomach rumbled loudly, and she grimaced. She always seemed to be hungry lately. In fact, skip lately. She was always hungry, full stop. Gemma guessed her passion for food was good news for a girl who earned her living running a baking business and writing recipe books, but it did make keeping the weight off bloody hard work. She'd lost quite a bit when she and Cal, her ex-footballer partner, had first moved to Kenniston to set up their business, but almost a year and a half on Gemma had noticed that her waistbands were getting a little snug again. She blamed Cal, whose bread and buns really were to die for, as well as her own dreadful habit of sampling whatever latest cake she was creating. Writing the book hadn't helped either. She must have put on a pound for every page! Thank God she'd stepped back from appearing on the show, Gemma thought. Apart from discovering that she actually didn't enjoy the attention fame brought with it, the old saying that television added ten pounds in weight was an understatement. There was no way Gemma wanted to be on national TV with all her fat bits on display. No way at all. She'd rather drown herself in a latte. A skinny one, obviously.

"Hungry, babe?" Angel, who seemed to live on a diet of fresh air and adrenalin, threw Gemma a sympathetic look. "I'm sorry we didn't stop for breakfast. Let's go and get something now and have a mooch round the shops." She glanced down at the watch on her slender wrist, something hugely expensive that Laurence had dug out of the rapidly emptying Elliott vault, and laughed, holding her arm up. "Typical Elliott family watch. I forgot it doesn't work – a bit like the rest of them! I haven't a clue what the time is but I'm sure it's time we got some grub."

Gemma looked at her own far more modest Baby-G. It was a present from Cal and she treasured it because it was one of the few things he'd bought her. Paying his monster tax bill and getting solvent had been his prime focus since he'd signed up for *Bread and Butlers*. He must be getting nearer the goal though: the business was thriving and even her own cake-making branch of it was turning a healthy profit. Maybe they'd soon be able to devote themselves to this one hundred percent and step right away from the television side of things.

"Earth to Gemma?" teased Angel. "The time?"

"Sorry! Sorry! It's almost noon."

"Great, that gives us bags of time," said Angel, shoving her Montblanc pen into an LV tote. "We're not due to film until seven, so I reckon we've got a couple of hours to enjoy Truro before we have to head back to Devon. Let's go and grab some lunch."

Flustered, Gemma returned her attention to the present. God, she kept doing this lately, drifting off into little daydreams and fantasies about the ideal life for her and Cal. One minute she was mixing the ingredients for a cake and the next she was miles away – maybe in a cottage surrounded by children with Cal's golden ringlets and her snub nose, or perhaps with Cal down on one knee and asking her the one question she was longing to hear. Gemma shook her head. She couldn't dwell on these thoughts; they only made her increasingly frustrated and impatient to move on with their lives. Like Cal had said only yesterday, she really needed to concentrate on the present, which right now meant packing away her things, saying goodbye to the bookshop staff and signing a couple more autographs for latecomers.

The signing well and truly over, Gemma wound her scarf tightly around her neck, shoved a hat onto her curly hair and put her sunglasses on. There, that was better. Now she was just an average shopper in the crowd, not Gemma the celebrity cake maker or the girlfriend of Callum South the legendary Premier League footballer, but just a rather plump girl dressed up for some Christmas shopping on a sunny December Saturday. Yes, the days of Gemma wanting fame were long gone. Now she enjoyed acting in an amateur group and was happy to let others have the limelight. Celebrity was, in Gemma's book, seriously overrated.

Unlike Angel, whose need to be recognised was almost as great as her need for oxygen, Gemma preferred to go incognito. She managed to achieve this most of the time but today with Angel, who was busy flicking her blonde extensions about and making a big show of putting her giant Bvlgaris on, she stood no chance. As the girls linked arms and wandered through the town, eyes followed them and people pointed and whispered excitedly. Gemma shrunk further into her coat and buried her nose in her scarf. Fame was no fun at all and, much as she knew it was going to upset Cal, she couldn't carry on like this for much longer.

She was going to have to make some changes.

Chapter 2

By the time they were seated on the top floor of a chic café – in the window, of course, so that Angel could be admired by everyone passing by below – Gemma had a good idea of how a goldfish might feel.

Once the waitress had delivered their coffees and food (Greek salad with no dressing for Angel, and a pasty the size of a tractor wheel for Gemma), the pace of the day seemed to slow. It had been a mad rush to get to Cornwall for nine and Gemma had been awake even earlier than Cal, who was always out of bed by dawn to get the day's baking under way. She'd nuzzled up to him hopefully, loving the warm scent of the skin between his shoulder blades, and dropped several kisses down his spine, but Cal had just clutched the duvet tightly and muttered something about sleeping. There were other things to do in bed apart from sleep, Gemma thought wistfully, but Cal seemed to have forgotten all about those. He was always exhausted and she completely understood why; juggling a filming schedule and the business was a crazy workload. Knowing this didn't make her feel much better though. There had been a time when Cal couldn't keep his hands off her...

"You're miles away today," Angel remarked. Her fork, loaded with glossy black olives and some healthy-looking green stuff, hovered over the plate before she lowered it. Gemma really admired that. She would have had to shovel it in and keep talking through her mouthful. Her pasty was already vanishing fast.

"What's wrong?" Angel asked. "You look really down."

How long did she have? Gemma wondered sadly. Besides, to Angel nothing was wrong: everything was perfect. The show was a hit, the bakery was a success, Cal was fast on his way to being solvent, they were generally happy (or as happy as two people who hardly had time to spend with one another anymore could be happy), she lived on a beautiful estate in Devon and she'd written a bestselling Christmas cookery book. Everything was great and Gemma wasn't even sure herself what the problem was. It wasn't anything she could pinpoint; rather, it was a nebulous twisting sensation deep in the pit of her stomach that something was out of synch. Instinct maybe, or intuition?

If she couldn't explain this to herself, Gemma knew there was no way she could make Angel understand. Besides, she felt ungrateful. Angel had worked her socks off to get *Bread and Butlers* off the ground and she lived for the show. Cal's paid tax bill and lessening debts, as well as the capital that had started their business, were all down to Angel.

Gemma shrugged and pushed her pasty away. Suddenly the congealing hunks of meat and slimy potato made her feel nauseous.

"Nothing. I'm fine."

With her extensions, false nails and designer bling, Gemma's best friend might look like a stereotypical airhead – but it was an unwise person who underestimated Angel Elliott. Her mind was as switched on as the Christmas lights strung across the high street. As soon as the words were out of her mouth, Gemma knew she had no hope of fooling her friend.

"That 'I'm fine' bollocks might work on Cal, but I'm not a bloke and therefore I know that 'I'm fine' actually means the exact opposite. You've hardly said a word all morning, you didn't even notice that fit bloke who wanted his book signed, and now you're not eating your lunch. Something's definitely up." Her blue eyes narrowed and she fixed Gemma with a stern look. "Come on; spill before CSI Cornwall sign me up!"

Gemma laughed. "What fit bloke?"

"You see? I knew there was something up!" squealed Angel. "How you could have missed him I'll never know! About six feet tall, white-blond hair, looked like Ryan Gosling's better-looking brother?"

Gemma thought back to the signing. There had been so many people there and she'd had half an eye on the doorway in case her parents showed up – not that this was particularly likely, because they were flat out with the farm – so she hadn't really been paying attention.

"Green gillet? Country boots?" prompted Angel, pulling a despairing face when Gemma still looked blank. "I give up with you, Gemma Pengelley. He was lush. I would!"

"You're a married woman!"

Angel grinned and returned to her salad. "So?" she said cheerfully through a mouthful of cos lettuce and feta. "That doesn't mean I can't look, does it? I love Laurence totally and utterly but I can still admire the finer specimens in God's great creation. Blimey, Gem. You don't think I've picked the builders at Kenniston for their bricklaying talents do you?"

To be honest Gemma hadn't taken much notice of the team of builders who'd been drafted in to start work on the mammoth project of restoring Laurence's ancestral home. Still, now she came to think about it she supposed they did look more like a collection of Calvin Klein models than the bum-cleavage-revealing, beer-bellied folk who tended to leer at her from their white vans.

"Good TV eye candy," Angel was saying sagely. "And Craig's been signed by Models 1 since he joined the show, which is good news.

There's always an opportunity if you look for it. It's what makes life so exciting."

Gemma stopped herself just in time from saying she'd be far more excited if Craig had spent less time posing for the film crew and a little more of it patching up the roof of the damp and gloomy gatehouse she and Cal shared. Angel lived and breathed Kenniston Hall and the show; she wouldn't have understood why Gemma was so weary of it all. In fairness Gemma hardly understood this herself. All she knew was that she was tired of having to constantly look over her shoulder in case the crew were lurking, and even more tired of never having Cal to herself. Surely the time was coming for them to step away from it all and concentrate on themselves? Cal kept saying that they needed the money but Gemma couldn't for the life of her imagine what for. Just how big were his tax bills?

To distract herself she pushed the pasty around a bit, but Angel wasn't fooled.

"OK, now I'm really worried. Not noticing hot guys is one thing; you not eating lunch is quite another. Is everything all right with you and Cal?"

Gemma abandoned any pretence of eating her food and pushed her plate away. Was everything all right with her and Cal? She thought it was, hoped it was, but how did you ever know for sure? How well could you ever really know somebody else? The lack of sex was down to his working so hard. Having cameras in tow – because Cal had signed a second contract when Gemma had retreated from the limelight – didn't exactly enhance your hopes of a love life, unless you were making a very different genre of television. Cal was still his usual cheerful, affectionate and loveable self but Gemma had the oddest feeling that he was holding something back. Was their lack of bedroom action a barometer? Did the few extra pounds she'd put on lately turn him off? She thought this highly unlikely, seeing as she'd been several stones heavier when they'd first got together and Cal hadn't been able to keep his hands off her then. Besides, he was hardly skinny himself! He had zero willpower when it came to food, so working in a bakery was proving far too tempting for Cal.

"Sure, and isn't it quality control?" he'd laugh, creases of good humour starring his eyes as he sampled a bit of brioche or maybe a slice of cheese loaf. Quite a bit of sampling went on in Cal's kitchen, judging by the constant loosening of notches on his belt, but Gemma didn't care – she loved every inch of him. Twelve stone or fifteen stone; it didn't matter to her. Callum South, with his golden shock of curly hair, sleepy downturned eyes the colour of Irish peat and huge appetite for all the good things in life, still made her legs turn to soggy string.

"We're fine," Gemma said eventually, because Angel was still waiting for a reply. She loved her friend but these days she was always wary of divulging too much. Angel was so driven that Gemma wouldn't put it past her to use any information for ratings. She was still smarting from the time the *Bread and Butlers* production team had thought it a good idea to lob Cal's glamour-model ex into an episode. Fifi Royale had a brain like Swiss cheese and boobs bigger than her head, but Cal had dated her and *FHM* had rated her at number four in their Britain's Sexiest chart. Cal had laughed and promised that Gemma was number one in Callum South's Sexiest chart, but even so it wasn't a nice situation to be in. Tricks like that were the brainchildren of the show's new producer, Dwayne, and Gemma hadn't been impressed. Dwayne was yet another reason why she hadn't signed up for a second season.

Angel regarded her thoughtfully. "Really? Things got better when you moved out of the main house, right?"

Living in Kenniston Hall had been fun to begin with, a bit like an extended sleepover, but after a while Gemma and Cal had been driven demented. Decamping to the Lion Lodge had seemed like a great idea. The pretty gatehouse was a mile from the Hall, overlooked one of Capability Brown's ornamental lakes and had a stunning view over rolling parkland and the wiggling ribbon drive to Kenniston. With its leaded windows, quirky little rooms and romantic open fires it had felt like one step closer to Gemma's dream home. Unfortunately though, the dream had soon become a nightmare. The house was all fur coat and no knickers. Capability Brown hadn't been quite so capable when he'd planned the lake, and damp seeped into every corner of the building. The drive was a quagmire when it rained (Gemma's Beetle was still abandoned halfway to the Hall), black mould coated most of the surfaces, and the fires belched smoke. The storage heaters had been on strike since about 1950 and consequently Gemma and Cal slept in tracksuits, thick socks and hoodies. It was hardly an environment conducive to ripping off clothes and exploring one another's naked bodies, Gemma reflected. They'd be in danger of getting frostbite. As it stood, the one and only serious argument they'd ever had had been over who'd mislaid the hot-water bottle.

There was no chance of the Elliotts spending money doing up the Lion Lodge, not when the Hall was in an even worse state. Gemma had wanted to rent a cottage in Rewe but Cal, keen to save money, had been all for moving back to the Hall. At least there he'd have been near his kitchen rather than wrecking the suspension on his beloved Range Rover by trundling up and down the rutted drive. In the end it came down to a choice between the slightly less Baltic conditions of the big house and the privacy of the Lion Lodge, which in Gemma's mind was no choice at all. She'd bought another hot-water bottle, some good-quality thermals and a fan heater, and kissed her love life goodbye until the spring.

"Gem?" Angel prompted, looking truly worried now. "Everything is OK with you guys, isn't it?"

Gemma didn't want to sound like she was moaning. She had a gorgeous partner and a great career, and she lived in a beautiful part of the world. She needed to look at the positives and be thankful for them, as her life-coach friend Dee would say.

"I think so. No, of course we are. It's just so busy and we're never on our own enough. There's always a crew member or one of Cal's team mates or," she paused and rolled her eyes, "even worse, one of Cal's family about. It's pretty hard to get some private time. God help me if his mother turns up again."

Of all the stresses in her life, Gemma thought that Cal's huge and boisterous family were probably right up there with calorie counting and playing dodge-the-falling-masonry whenever she stepped outside the gatehouse. Cal had so many siblings it felt as though hardly a month went by when one of the South clan wasn't visiting. No wonder she and Cal never had time for sex. And when Cal's mother came to stay it was a total no-no. Mammy South was a devout Catholic, had a saint for just about everything and was horrified that her beloved eldest son was living in sin with a Protestant. Even Casanova would have been put off nookie with Mammy South clicking her rosary beads on the other side of the bedroom wall.

"Hmm," said Angel. Was it her imagination, Gemma wondered, or did her best friend look a bit shifty? "Maybe you could get more involved with the show again?" Angel suggested hopefully. "That way you'd see Cal more."

Gemma smiled. "You don't give up, do you? How many times do I need to say it? I'm through with TV. I just want to concentrate on the cakes and being with Cal. I know it's not very PC but I just want our own place, a red Aga, a couple of kids and a normal life. I don't want to be famous."

"So much for feminism," said Angel, forking a bit more salad in.

Gemma chose to ignore this comment. So wanting to get married and have children wasn't a very feminist ambition; she could probably live with that. Anyway, running her own very successful cake-making business and writing a bestselling cookery book seemed pretty feminist to her. Besides, wasn't that the whole point of equality anyway? Women could have it all?

If they could figure out what "it all" was, of course.

"Cal's signed until the end of December," Angel reminded her, interrupting Gemma's rather philosophical train of thought. "Anton's really keen he signs again – and you too, of course. I really think you should. Another year isn't long, Gem."

Anton Yuri was the main shareholder in Seaside Rock, Angel's production company, and a Russian businessman so tough he made Putin look cuddly. Gemma wasn't keen to fall out with him – she didn't think being buried in a flyover would suit her – but she was even less keen to put up with another year of cameras and chaos.

She shook her head. "No way. I've told you, Angel, I'm really through with all that. Besides, I'm thirty in two weeks' time. It's time for a change."

"Don't say the 'T' word!" Angel, still a while away from the dreaded milestone birthday herself, shrank back as though the number was contagious.

Gemma shrugged. "There's no point hiding from it."

"There's every point hiding from it! Why do you think Crème de la Mer make so much money? Anyway, you're only as old as you feel."

In that case she was probably about one hundred and thirty, Gemma reflected gloomily. She felt tired and grumpy, and even if she bathed in Crème de la Mer she didn't think that would change.

"Do you want us to throw you a party?" Angel's face was bright with enthusiasm. Salad forgotten about, she reached for her iPhone to start making notes. "We could feature it in one of the next episodes. Do you fancy hiring a fairground like that guy from One Direction did for his girlfriend?" Her finger hovered over the touchscreen. "We could ask his management who organised it."

"I hate fairground rides," Gemma reminded Angel. "I got sick on *It's a Small World* when I went on the school trip to Euro Disney."

"Ok then, how about fancy dress? That could be fun. We could have a theme."

Only somebody who was slim and gorgeous could possibly think fancy dress was fun. Such parties normally threw Gemma into a total panic, as she not only had to come up with a costume but also one that hid her fat bits and didn't give her cleavage Jordan would kill for. Add to this the horror of being paraded before the entire nation and

Gemma thought she'd rather spend a night saying Hail Marys with Mammy South.

It was time to nip this in the bud before Angel got totally carried away and booked the Middletons to plan the party.

"I'm having a low-key birthday," she said firmly. "Just Cal and me."

"Spoilsport," said Angel. "Be like that then. I was only trying to do something nice."

"And boost your ratings," said Gemma.

Angel raised her hands in mock surrender. "You've got me. But it could still have been fun. Being thirty is bad enough, in my opinion, and having a big party and lots of booze could take some of the sting out of it. When it's my thirtieth Laurence had better do something spectacular to take my mind off it, that's all I can say. He's got enough time to plan it."

"I just want to be alone with Cal," Gemma sighed. In the back of her mind an idea was starting to form, and she began to feel excited. But before she explored this any further she knew she had to make it very clear to Angel that she didn't want the kind of party that would make one of Elton John's seem modest. She gave her best friend a stern look. "I don't want any secret parties. Not one. I mean it, OK?"

Angel nodded, her attention diverted now by several people down in the street who were pointing eagerly up at the café window. She gave them a wave and a megawatt smile. Gemma gave up. Her best friend would never understand. She sipped her coffee thoughtfully and began to piece a plan together. She only hoped that Cal wasn't thinking along the same lines, because that could make life tricky.

Angel, having finished waving, was busy tapping away on her pink iPhone.

"Laurence," she explained, when Gemma glanced over. "Don't panic; I'm not tweeting pictures of us. He's missing me and wants to know when we'll be back."

Laurence texted Angel non-stop. Gemma couldn't work out if this was romantic or just bloody irritating. In any case the iPhone chimed at regular intervals and usually caused Angel to giggle or blush. The two were certainly devoted, that was for certain, and Cal was always moaning that filming often got delayed because they kept sneaking off to snatch an hour's nookie. There was no doubt that Angel had melted Laurence's frosty aristocratic reserve. The episode when he'd sexted his mother by mistake had been hilarious. Not a lot ever shocked Daphne Elliott, apart from the hunting ban, and her no-nonsense reaction had been TV gold. Laurence had been red-faced for a day or two – but judging by the way Angel was now giggling and typing like crazy, he hadn't been put off.

Gemma sighed. The Elliotts were so loved up, and although comparisons were odious she couldn't help examining her own relationship in the glittering light of theirs. She really needed to do something to spice up her love life – and this was where her brilliant idea could come in. Fishing her own phone out of her Seasalt bag, Gemma's heart lifted to see a text from Cal. See! They might not be bonking each other's brains out non-stop but they had a bond, a true understanding that went far deeper than the physical. He was thinking about her just as much as Laurence was thinking about Angel. Smiling, she opened the message.

Don't forget to bring back a real Cornish pasty

Oh.

That summed things up perfectly, didn't it? Laurence sent Angel flirtatious and cheeky messages, whereas Cal just put in an order for supper. Something had to change and soon.

"What's the matter with you?" Angel asked. Her cheeks were flushed and her eyes glittered like one of Asprey's window displays. It was the look of a woman whose partner hadn't just texted to ask her to visit the pasty shop.

Gemma slid the phone across the table. "You asked me how things were with Cal? I think this probably says it all."

Angel scanned the text and shook her head. "Come on babe, that's just Cal. You know he loves his food. Didn't you guys meet in a pasty shop?"

This was true. Gemma had knocked Cal flying and his buns and sausage rolls had flown everywhere. Their mutual hatred of diets and love of cooking had certainly brought them together.

"Things haven't been very romantic lately," Gemma confessed. She didn't want to tell Angel too much but maybe her friend would have some ideas? Laurence was certainly not thinking about pasties when he texted his wife.

Angel's eyes widened. "Oh!"

"I know he's tired," Gemma said, feeling horribly disloyal. Cal would hate to think she'd been discussing their sex life with Angel. "And I know that the Lion Lodge isn't the most romantic setting. It's cold and damp for a start. Maybe that puts him off?"

"Bollocks," said Angel sharply. "Kenniston's bloody arctic and that doesn't stop us. Best way to keep warm. Throw out that hot-water bottle, that's my advice, then Cal will have to give you some action or freeze to death."

The thought of parting with the hot-water bottle in mid December was enough to bring Gemma out in a rash.

"It's fine," she said quickly, because Angel had that look on her face, the look that meant she was cooking up an idea. Gemma knew that expression far too well. She'd seen it the day Angel had decided they should abandon London living and run away to Cornwall for the summer, and she'd seen it too when *Bread and Butlers* had been dreamed up. It was time to distract her friend before she invited a TV sex therapist to stay at Kenniston, or something equally embarrassing.

"I'm just moaning," she insisted quickly. "It really is fine."

"Don't fib to me," said Angel sternly. "I'm not your boyfriend."

Gemma shrugged. "All couples go through phases like this."

Angel looked like she didn't believe this for a second. She bit her full bottom lip thoughtfully for a moment and then clapped her hands.

"Eureka! I've got the solution! I feel like Pythagoras did in the bath!"

"Archimedes," Gemma corrected. "Pythagoras was triangles."

Angel rolled her eyes. "Triangles, baths, whatever. Who cares? What matters, Gem, is that I have had a brilliant idea that's guaranteed to put the spice back into your love life."

Placing a twenty-pound note onto the table, she jumped to her feet and picked up her bag while Gemma stared at her with a growing sense of doom. It was too late: Angel was up and running with a plan.

"Come on, then! Don't just sit there!" cried Angel when Gemma didn't budge.

"Where are we going?" Gemma asked, warily.

But Angel just tapped her nose and winked. "Somewhere that will help you give Cal more than a cream horn! Trust me, it'll be brilliant! Now come on!"

Fired up, her friend was already heading down the narrow stairs and out into the Christmas crowds. With a sinking heart, Gemma gathered up her bag and coat and followed her. Like it or not, it seemed that her love life was now well and truly in Angel's beautifully manicured hands.

Chapter 3

"Pulse? This is your brilliant idea?"

Gemma stood on the pavement outside the Truro store, certain that her face was as red as the sexy Mrs Santa outfits in the window. All around her a tide of shoppers flowed through the town and she was dreadfully aware that her mother's WI friends were probably among them. Cornwall was a surprisingly small place and Demelza Pengelley would know that her daughter was in a, shock horror, sex shop, before you could say buzzing bunny.

"Like duh! Of course!" Angel looked thrilled with herself. "Where else do you go when you want to spice up your love life?"

"A sex shop?" Gemma was poised to flee. Oh God! Was that Mrs Tremaine from the neighbouring farm, just crossing the road? And what if her old English teacher came wandering by? She'd just die!

"Sex shop? What century are you in?" Angel grinned. "Haven't you read *Fifty Shades of Grey*? This is all mainstream now."

Actually Gemma hadn't read the infamous bestseller – and she didn't intend to, either. Call her old fashioned, but whipping didn't really do it for her (unless you counted whipping cream for the delicious melt-in-the-mouth éclairs she made), and after several bossy boyfriends, being dominated held about as much appeal as tucking into a bowl of vomit. No, when it came to her reading material, Gemma was a Mills and Boon girl. She wanted her brooding alpha male and to be swept off her feet, but she'd rather he did it in a sumptuous boudoir full of drifting muslin drapes and plump cushions than in a room of pain – red or any other colour. Oh dear. Did that make her boring? Was that the problem? Was Cal bored?

She glanced at the window display. It all looked innocent enough from the safety of the pavement. The lingerie was frilly and cheeky and the fluffy handcuffs seemed rather fun. Gemma supposed that if she handcuffed Cal to the bed he couldn't wander off to try out that new recipe for focaccia he'd just thought of. Much as she loved her baking, taking second place to a loaf was rather insulting.

"Pulse is fun! It's supposed to empower women," said Angel, sensing that her friend was weakening. She tugged Gemma's arm hopefully. "It can't hurt to just have a little look, can it? They do all kinds of stuff in there. Even chocolate body paint. I bet Cal would love that."

Gemma laughed. Angel wasn't wrong. "He'd eat the lot out the jar with a spoon before it ever made it to the bedroom."

The door of the shop opened and two girls burst into the street, giggling and clutching lilac-coloured bags. They looked thrilled with their purchases and nobody outside batted an eyelid.

"See?" said Angel. "Shopping here is fun. There's not a raincoat-wearing perv in sight, I promise. This is just a giggle, Gem, and the lingerie is gorgeous." Her eyes took on the gleam of a religious fanatic. "Actually, I wonder if I could design a range for them? What do you think?"

What Gemma thought was *Oh crap!* That really was Mrs Tremaine across the road, and she was heading this way right now. In approximately ten seconds' time she'd be within eyeball-touching distance and Gemma's poor mum would never be able to look the church flower-arranging committee members in the eye again. Everyone in the village would know that her daughter was a hussy. People had long memories where Gemma came from, and her mother's shame would be complete.

To Angel's joy, Gemma shot forwards like a horse out of the starting gate and burst through the door and into the shop. Goodness, this must be exactly how Alice felt when she fell down the rabbit hole. There was even a giant bunny-style vibrator on a pedestal, surrounded by hundreds of his smaller siblings in a mind-boggling array of sizes and colours. The shop was dark and intimate, almost womblike, and lit beautifully so that all the products were easy to see and looked gorgeous. Christmas had certainly arrived here too: the festive theme was everywhere. Gemma's eyes were out on stalks. Who ever knew that Santa's Little Helper did *that*? And why were bits cut out of those pants? And call that scrap of lace a bra? You'd freeze wearing this lingerie at the Lion Lodge; some trusty old M&S thermals were much more useful!

"You are young in the ways of the Force," sighed Angel, grabbing Gemma's arm and steering her through the displays. She had a basket on her arm and was now merrily lobbing items in.

"A naughty teacher's outfit?" Gemma said doubtfully. "I'm not sure that's going to help. Cal left school at sixteen."

"Don't look so worried," Angel said. "This isn't all for you. Laurence deserves some presents too. The teacher outfit will drive him wild. It's a public-schoolboy thing."

"Too much information," Gemma said, pulling a face. She glanced about the shop. "Look, can't I just buy some frilly pants or something?" The underwear all seemed miniscule anyway; she'd look like the Pillsbury Doughboy caught cross-dressing, which was hardly going to turn Cal on, no matter how much he loved baking. "Maybe we should go to Evans?"

"Trust me," said Angel, a phrase that always put Gemma on red alert. Fighting the growing feeling that this was a very bad idea indeed, she joined Angel over by the sexy Santa outfits. Her friend was flipping through the rails until she located a size that Gemma thought might just about cover her bum cheeks. Angel held the costume up against her friend, narrowing her eyes, then nodded sagely and added it to the collection.

"Perfect."

"Really?" Gemma wasn't convinced. "It looks a bit small. I don't think I'll fit in."

"That, my dear innocent one, is the point," Angel said patiently. "You don't wear this to Waitrose, Gem. You wear it in the bedroom."

Gemma thought that if she wore this in their bedroom she'd die of hypothermia. Cal said every time he nipped to the loo he felt like Captain Oates. Still, sometimes it was easier just to let Angel do her thing. Following her friend around the store, she let her select some red and green Christmas underwear, a set of Santa-style handcuffs, a red crop which The Pony Club would have never allowed, and some glittery edible body paint. She drew the line at a festive-style bunny though.

Gemma wasn't a prude. She'd had vibrators in the past, usually as a daft presents or bought when several sheets to the wind on pink wine and at a hen party (and she'd even carted one to Rock because she'd thought her love life was over back then), but to actually buy one and present it to Cal as a festive treat? The very idea made her feel faint. Oh dear. Maybe she was less liberated than she thought?

Gemma held the bright red contraption nervously. It wiggled and jiggled cheerfully in her hand but quite frankly all she wanted to do was call the RSPCA. Why on earth had the designers given it a cute little face and sweet little ears? That was just wrong! It needed to be eating carrots and living in a hutch, not going... there!

"No way," she said firmly.

"You're mad," shrugged Angel, "but up to you. Laurence bought me one when he had to go on a stag weekend; Ludo somebody or other, I think it was. Posh people really do have silly names. Anyway, bringing Bugs home was the worst mistake he ever made!" She started to cackle at the memory and several other shoppers looked up and gave her a conspiratorial smile. Then recognition dawned on their faces and before Gemma knew what was happening they'd whipped out their mobiles and were taking pictures.

Taking pictures of her clutching a vibrator.

Gemma had the hideous sensation that she was in a lift and descending very, very fast. Those pictures would be all over the social media by the time she even reached the till, and the celebrity magazines would go mad. Oh God! What if her mother saw the pictures? Or even worse, Cal?

"Chill out," was Angel's advice when Gemma pointed out what had happened. "Breathe, Gemma. It's a couple of blurry selfies that they'll probably forget about. Besides, this is the twenty-first century. And if the worst comes to the worst maybe we'll get a deal out of it? You could be the new Pulse poster girl! It's got to be more fun than baking cakes."

Gemma wasn't amused. It was all very well for Angel. She had a knack for falling in the stinky brown stuff and still coming up smelling of Coco Mademoiselle, whereas Gemma just ended up needing a good bath. Hoping that the girls were more interested in Angel than in her anyway, she followed her friend to the checkout.

"This is on me," Angel insisted, handing over Laurence's well-worn credit card. "I'll take one of these as well," she told the shop assistant as she picked up a copy of *Fifty Shades*. "Don't argue, Gemma. Call it an early Christmas present. Fingers crossed it'll spice up your Yuletide."

Gemma doubted it. As soon as she was home this lot was getting shoved to the back of the deepest darkest cupboard she could find. The book might be handy for kindling. There was no way she was prancing around dressed like something from a nineteen-nineties' Mariah Carey Christmas video. No way at all.

"Thanks," she said politely, taking the carrier bag.

"Don't thank me until you've tried it," said Angel. "I know you, Gemma Pengelley! You're planning to shove that bag somewhere and forget all about it, aren't you?"

Gemma stared at her. "Are you psychic?"

"No, I just know you. But remember you wanted to try and spice things up again, and having fun is the best way. Don't take any of this seriously. It's just a bit of a giggle. It can't hurt to give it a try."

Privately Gemma thought that the damage to her self-esteem when Cal saw her dressed as sexy Mrs Santa and gave himself a hernia laughing could be fatal. Even worse, what if all her fat bits turned him off totally? The outfit was a size twelve but Gemma knew in her heart that she was more like a fourteen these days. It was living in the Lion Lodge. She was eating to keep warm. And entertain herself. And comfort herself.

Something had to change. She couldn't go on like this.

Outside now in the sharp cold air, the girls rejoined the Christmas crowds. Angel threaded her arm through Gemma's and together they strolled along the high street, listening to the carols and peering in at the festive shop windows. The air was thick with the aromas of roasting chestnuts and mulled wine from the market vendors, and the excitement of the shoppers was palpable. This was what Christmas was all about. There was nowhere like Cornwall for Christmas. Devon was lovely but it wasn't home; Gemma missed her native county more and more every day. She wanted to visit the Lanhydrock Christmas shop and toast her toes in front of the log fire, meander with Cal through the Cothele Christmas Food Fair and pick out a few goodies to try. She wanted to wake up with him on Christmas Day and walk on the beach. She wanted to go home for Christmas.

And that was when her brilliant idea finally took shape. It was no longer just a nebulous mass of ifs and maybes; now it was solidifying and appearing before her very eyes, becoming more real with every second. It was so simple and so obvious that Gemma laughed out loud. Of course! The solution had been there all along. Coming back to Cornwall had just made it clear.

It was time she took matters into her own hands. Forget the silly costumes and the fluffy handcuffs, buzzing bunnies and glittery body paints.

Gemma had a much better idea of how to give Cal a Christmas to remember.

Chapter 4

Leaving Cornwall was always hard, but for some reason Gemma couldn't quite fathom it was getting even harder. Maybe it was a coming-up-for-thirty thing? Getting away from the sticks and heading for the bright lights of London had once been her biggest dream. When she was sixteen you'd hardly have seen her for the cloud of dust on the A30. Theatres, shops, the Tube – all these things had beckoned, and for a while it had all been great fun. There'd been her time at the BRIT School, which had been brilliant, then a few TV roles and a bit of theatre too, as well as all kinds of parties and craziness. But somewhere along the line something had shifted and Gemma had found herself longing for Cornwall's lemon-sharp air, broad light and ever-changing sea, as sludgy as the Thames one moment and Caribbean blue the next. That wonderful summer in Rock had only confirmed what Gemma had long suspected, that Cornwall was etched deep into her soul, written through her like a stick of Looe rock, and that it was only when she was back over the Tamar that she'd feel at home again.

East Devon was lovely too and she was lucky to live there, Gemma reminded herself sternly as Angel backed the Land Rover Defender out of the narrow parking space they'd been lucky enough to find, right at the furthest end of the Tesco car park. How Angel could see was anyone's guess; the back seat was piled high with carrier bags and parcels, her best friend having been determined to make inroads into her Christmas shopping. Gemma closed her eyes in terror. When she opened them again they were on the ring road and heading out of town, past the spires of the cathedral as it drowsed in the afternoon sunshine, and following the road that hugged the bank of the river. The water sparkled as it danced out into the sea. Seagulls clotted the sky, circling high up in the chilly air, and their calls could even be heard above the engine. They brought to mind images of sunnier times, of picnics, stripy windbreaks and thick wedges of golden beach.

What was to stop her and Cal moving to Cornwall once he'd finished with *Bread and Butlers*? Gemma wondered idly. The bakery could relocate; Pengelley's Cakes could be made anywhere in the UK, and if they stayed away from the trendy areas like Rock they'd get more for their money. Cal was always on about how much they needed to watch the pennies. It was one of the reasons he worked so hard, and having squandered more than Gemma would ever earn in a lifetime she guessed he knew what he was talking about. They could buy a little place down here, maybe find a way of linking up with Prince Charles's organic Duchy Originals range, and begin a whole new life. She could see it now: the pretty cottage they'd buy, the big kitchen complete with the red Aga she'd always longed for and a squashy sofa, and upstairs a massive sleigh bed with snowy white pillows, mounds of duvets and not a patch of mould in sight. OK, so maybe there would be a little bit of mould somewhere; Cornwall was a damp county after all. And the white pillows might suffer as a consequence of Gemma's habit of eating toast and Marmite in bed. Nevertheless, as fantasies went this was a great one – much more up her street than dressing up in a sexy Santa costume and walloping Cal with a red crop. Maybe she was boring, but Gemma felt a lot more excited about filling her imaginary kitchen with mugs and Le Creuset cookware than she did about the contents of the Pulse bag.

"Can we make a detour before we head home?" Gemma asked Angel. Her idea was mutating now, taking on a life all of its own. It was the same delicious and tingly sensation she had when she knew that she'd totally nailed a cake recipe.

Angel, who was weaving in and out of the busy Christmas-shopping traffic with a skill that Lewis Hamilton would envy, threw her a curious look.

"Not to Rock is it, babes? I know you'd like to see Dee but it's a bit out of our way – and besides, the place will be dead this time of year."

"No, it's nowhere near as far as Rock. I know you have to be back to shoot this evening. This'll only take an extra half an hour or so, I promise."

"Now I'm intrigued," said Angel. "What is it? A designer pasty shop? Are we on a mission to carry out industrial espionage? Watch out Ginsters; we're coming to get you?"

"First of all, as a self-respecting Cornish maid I don't consider a Ginsters to be a real pasty," Gemma told her sternly, "and secondly I don't just think about food, you know. I wanted to have a look at this cottage I know. It's not far; it's just beyond Bodmin, on the edge of Dad's farm."

"Any particular reason?"

"Just curiosity really. It's ever so pretty, right on a little creek that flows into the River Fowey. It's been derelict for as long as I can remember – my brothers and I used to play there as kids – and I've always wondered whether it would be possible to do something with it."

"Sounds cool," said Angel. She checked her watch and groaned. "I have *so* got to get this bloody thing fixed. I don't care that it's an heirloom; what's the use if it doesn't work?"

"It's just gone two," said Gemma. Her Baby-G might not date from the reign of Louis XIV or whoever, but at least it worked.

"Fab." Angel grinned at her. "Magical mystery tour, here we come!"

The road to Penmerryn Creek was every bit as twisty and turny as Gemma remembered. From the relative speed and normality of the A30 it was a shock to be plunged into the sunken lanes that laced together numerous small Cornish villages and hamlets. At this time of year the trees were bare, their limbs reaching into the Wedgwood-blue sky like stark fingers, and patterns of winter sun dappled the tarmac. Horses wrapped in thick rugs stood waiting hopefully in muddy gateways with their breath rising in smoky plumes, and cows huddled against the hedgerows. That was her father's herd, Gemma thought, instinctively assessing them. They looked good for the winter: healthy enough to still yield milk and make it through the dark cold days before another meeting with Henry, the prize bull. She craned her neck and, sure enough, there Henry was, all alone in the next field, sporting his gold nose ring like a gansta rappa. He was a chunky mountain of a beast with the sex drive of a premier footballer (Cal being the exception to the rule here, unfortunately) and all the finesse of a wrecking ball. With his beady eyes and thick neck he reminded Gemma of Mr Yuri. She gulped nervously. Persuading Cal to step away from the show was going to be harder than she'd thought. If Anton Yuri took exception it would be concrete-boots time for sure.

The lane ended rather abruptly at a T-junction and Angel paused the car here, waiting for directions – but Gemma was still distracted by the view. The empty fields rolling away on the right were evidence of wheat and maize long harvested and put away for the winter months. Past these and stretching to the horizon were endless acres of corduroy plough hemmed with green set-aside; from a distance, it looked like a giant had opened a packet of chocolate limes and scattered them across the landscape. Gemma knew every inch of this land, every ditch and boggy patch and dry-stone wall, because this was the farm that belonged to her family. Just over the brow of the hill, nestled from the wind by a copse of gnarled trees, was the old stone farmhouse. Chickens would be scratching in the yard and a grinder would be screeching away from one of the barns as repairs were made to machinery. Meanwhile, inside the farmhouse a hearty stew would be bubbling away on the range and Radio Four would be chatting away to itself. Penmerryn Farm. Home.

"Which way now, babes?" asked Angel. She peered nervously at the road in front. To the right it was fairly well maintained, but to the left a thick spine of greenery ran down the centre of the asphalt; it reminded her of a stegosaurus. "Please say right. I know I'm in a four-by-four but I'm not really up for off-roading."

"Sorry, it's left," Gemma told her. "It'll be fine though. There's only a mile or so to go."

Angel let up the clutch and Gemma's heart began to thud with a heady cocktail of excitement and dread. The lane looked relatively unused, which had to be a good sign. If nobody was using the road then the cottage was still empty. And if the cottage was still empty then maybe, just maybe, she could persuade Cal to buy it? If his memories of the place were anything like hers then Gemma just knew he wouldn't be able to resist it either.

"So where exactly are we going?" Angel asked. The lane was dropping now at some rate and she touched the brakes several times rather anxiously. The trees either side of the lane had knitted together over the years. In the summer Gemma knew that it would be the most beautiful emerald canopy through which speckles of light would dance and play. The now skeletal hedgerows would be verdant and starred with ox-eye daisies or plumed with valerian. On a mid-December afternoon, though, it felt as if they were driving into a bony cage, and Gemma shivered in spite of the heated seats in the car. She hoped that her memories of the last time she'd visited, a kaleidoscope of images as brightly coloured as any of the prints sold in the nearby gift shops and galleries, weren't influenced by the heat of the midsummer sun and the whisper of Cal's lips against her throat…

"Hello? Earth to Gemma? Where exactly are we going?" Angel changed down another gear. "Thank God for four-wheel drive. I thought we were looking at a cottage, not going on a Land Rover safari! This is like driving down Everest!"

Gemma raised her eyebrows in despair. "Stop being such a townie! This is nothing; it's more of a slope than a hill. The cottage is just at the bottom. It's on a creek which leads to the River Fowey, so that's why we're going downhill."

"Bit inconvenient," said Angel, which was ironic in the supreme, coming from a woman who lived at Kenniston Hall – which although beautiful and historically significant had to be the most inconvenient place in the world, in Gemma's opinion. Boiling kettles to fill the bath was not her idea of fun. And if the Domino's deliveryman got the Stag Gate and the Lion Gate confused, you went very hungry indeed.

Anyway, this cottage wasn't about being convenient. It was about being the right place for her and Cal to make a proper start on their life together. The closer the car got the more Gemma's stomach started to pancake-flip. Any moment now and the car would break out of the trees; then they would pull up by the shimmering waters of the creek. This was where Penmerryn Cottage slumbered, half forgotten while the river and the seasons changed. It was a tumbledown boatman's dwelling, where she and her brothers had played as children. Later on, as teenagers, they'd camped here with friends during the endless summer holidays, drinking scrumpy and swimming in the cool river. It was a place apart from the rush of the outside world and somewhere the press and the cameras would never come looking. Somewhere they could put down roots and build a future.

This place was perfect for her and Cal. Gemma just knew it.

She'd always known it.

Earlier in the year she and Cal had managed to wangle a rare few days away from the business. The show had been on a break and Cal's deputy baker, Adam, had been itching for the chance to prove himself. So they'd packed a bag and hopped into Cal's Range Rover on a road trip. The sense of freedom as they'd driven out of the Lion Gate and headed towards the sinking sun had been intoxicating. They'd laughed and chatted non-stop, the tension of work slipping away with every mile that fell behind them. They'd made an adventure of the journey and had ended up staying at random bed and breakfasts along the route, Cal joking that by the time they crossed the Tamar he'd be dreaming in chintz and have an urge to build a fine collection of china figurines.

The final stop on their mini road trip had been a night with Gemma's parents, which saw Cal sleeping in the guest room and Gemma safely tucked up in her old teenage bedroom. Tiptoeing around in the dead of night at Penmerryn Farm was not a good idea, because the house had an intricate network of creaky floorboards that needed negotiating in the style of Catherine Zeta-Jones in *Entrapment* and, more importantly, because farmers tended to be up at the oddest hours.

The next afternoon Gemma's mother had packed for them a Famous Five style picnic of hardboiled eggs and doorstep sandwiches of crusty homemade bread, thick yellow butter and chunks of ham, and Gemma and Cal had headed off for a walk.

It had been a perfect English summer's day. The sky had been a cloudless, duck-egg blue and the air had trembled with the calls of wood pigeons. In the distance a combine harvester had been trawling a sea of wheat, and as Gemma and Cal had walked down the lane hand in hand, two riders had clopped past, tinting the air with the smell of citronella and hot horse. A heat haze had shimmered ahead of them – or maybe, Gemma had thought, this was the attraction between her and Cal, visible only to them and hotter than the parched earth beneath their feet. In the distance, the river had been sparkling in its hilly cleavage, the water shining brightly and calling them to come and swim.

"Jaysus, is there much farther to go?" Cal had grumbled, but the twinkle in his eye had shown he wasn't really complaining. "The picnic basket's bloody heavy, so it is. Your mammy's gone mad."

"She loves feeding people up," Gemma had said, poking her own midriff ruefully. "It's just as well we're only here for a short time."

"You look gorgeous: good enough to eat," Cal had told her. "Never mind the fecking food; I want to nibble you!" And then he'd put the hamper down, folded Gemma in his arms and kissed her so long and hard that by the time they broke apart food had been the last thing on either of their minds.

Then Gemma had had a brainwave and, grabbing Cal's hand, had steered him through a scalped cornfield, along a shady bridleway and finally out through the dense knot of trees to a crumbling shell of a boatman's cottage that was drowsing near the cool blue water of the creek. The granite walls were smothered in ivy and embroidered with convolvulus, and apart from the warning cry of a blackbird the place was completely still. An old rowing boat was pulled up on the mudflats and a jetty listed drunkenly beside it, black stumps of wood still embedded in the silt like rotting teeth in a neglected mouth. The air was rich with the smell of salt and wild garlic, and the sun was hot on their skin.

"Jaysus," Cal had breathed, drawing Gemma alongside him and holding her close. "What a stunning place."

"Do you like it?" Her heart had seemed to wait for him to reply before it could beat again. Penmerryn was one of her most treasured secrets, and she wanted so much for Cal to feel the magic too that it almost hurt.

Cal had gazed around him. His eyes, when they'd met hers, had been bright with wonder. "It's fecking amazing, Gem. Magical, so it is."

Of course he got it. He was Cal. He totally got her too.

Hand in hand they'd explored the place, clambering over the fallen rafters and peering up the chimneys into the blue sky beyond. Then, like children, they'd stripped to their underwear and plunged into the chilly creek, shrieking at the icy water and splashing each other until they were soaked.

"Come over here," Cal had said to Gemma.

He was standing in the middle of the creek now, his face split with a huge grin and his curly hair beaded with droplets. Gemma had swum towards him, a leisurely breaststroke rather than her usual slicing crawl, then looped her arms over his neck and wound her legs around his waist. She'd felt his hardness in spite of the cold water and shivered.

Cal's eyelashes had been starred with water droplets and his strong shoulders were dusted with cinnamon freckles. He'd pulled her closer and rubbed his nose against hers.

"I love you, Gemma Pengelley," he'd said. "More than I ever knew I could ever love anyone."

He'd kissed her then and they'd sunk under the water, surfacing again afterwards with gasps of laughter.

"Come on," Gemma had said. "I'll race you! Last one back sorts the picnic!"

This had hardly been a fair challenge. Cal was a dreadful swimmer (he'd barely mastered a splashy kind of doggy paddle), whereas Gemma had been the school champion. But the water was shallow, and within seconds they'd been staggering onto the weed-strewn riverbank. Gemma had been just about to do a victory dance when Cal had shot past her.

"Last one back to the house," he'd called over his shoulder.

Now who wasn't playing fair? Cal might have quit professional football and been a few stone overweight, but he still had an athlete's speed. Gemma could no more catch him up than she could fly to the moon.

"That's cheating," she'd complained when she'd joined him inside the cottage.

"I won, which means I'm the victor and I get to claim my reward." Cal had put his hands on his hips and given Gemma a look that had dusted her with goosebumps, even though she was standing in the bright sunshine. "Now, me darlin', how about we get you out of those wet things? You'll catch your death, so you will."

He'd stepped forward and unhooked her bra with one hand. Just how did boys learn to do that? Gemma had wondered. Was there a special class they had to go to at school? Then Cal's mouth had been on hers and all thought had been rendered useless as she'd melted into him. He'd lowered her tenderly onto the tartan car blanket that the Pengelleys had used for years as a picnic rug, and as his lips had travelled from the tender skin of her neck to her breasts, the scratchy wool and the hard edge of a twig pressing into her bottom had become just as much a part of the pleasure. The birdsong, the blue sky above the rafters and the smell of honeysuckle and garlic flowers had all mingled with the sensation of his lips and hands, and the vision of the brown eyes flecked with gold that held her own. Every movement had been bliss and every touch had sent her spinning and shimmering to a place she'd never thought she would find.

Later – much later, as the sun had begun to slide behind the jagged roof and the house martins had dived above them – Cal and Gemma had tucked into their picnic. Even though the bread had been curling, the ham had been dry and the Coke had been warm, nothing had ever tasted so good.

"I wish we could stay here forever," Gemma had sighed, resting her head on Cal's shoulder. "No crews butting in, no alarms; just you and me."

"We could build a bakery here," Cal had nodded. "Sure, and wouldn't that outhouse be a grand spot for it?"

"And over there is my kitchen, for the cakes." Gemma had pointed towards the back of the house. "The afternoon sun lights it beautifully.

A glass roof would be perfect here, so that I can lean against my red Aga and watch it set over the river."

"Red Aga?" Cal had dropped a kiss onto her nose. "Why red?"

Gemma had shrugged. "Just a crazy dream, I guess. I saw one once in a magazine and it seemed like a cosy colour."

"Then you shall have one," Cal had declared. "And I'll have a boat. We'll rebuild that jetty too."

And they'd sat curled into one another, imagining the wonderful things they could do with the house, until the shadows had pooled around them and the bats had begun flitting above their heads. The walk home had been quiet and reflective, their kisses tender rather than urgent now, and by the time she'd fallen into her narrow single bed, Gemma's eyes had been closing. The next day had been the drive back to Kenniston and the world of schedules, early starts and filming, but their perfect afternoon had stayed fresh in her mind. Sometimes all she needed was to smell wild garlic and she was right back in the ramshackle cottage, safe in Cal's arms and with his soft Irish voice spinning her those magical tales.

Maybe they didn't have to be tales? As the Defender bumped down the final stretch of rutted track that led to the cottage, Gemma was fizzing with excitement. This cottage was going to be for her and Cal. They'd be so happy here. It was meant to be.

"Oh!" Angel exclaimed, pulling on the handbrake so hard that the car almost span. "There's somebody already here. Look, there's a BMW parked up. And didn't you say the place was a ruin? It looks to me like someone's been really busy doing it up."

And just like that, all of Gemma's happy dreams came tumbling down around her ears, as though Fate had pulled the crucial block from her Jenga-like tower of secret hopes. Balanced on the window ledge of what Gemma had imagined might one day be her kitchen, and leaning against the brand new sparkling glass, was a sign. A sign that read *SOLD.*

Chapter 5

Gemma was disappointed but hardly surprised. Of course the cottage had been snapped up. Perhaps she ought to be astonished that it hadn't been sold years ago to some enterprising property developer. After all, wasn't Cornwall one of the most expensive places in the UK now? The Jamie Oliver and Rick Stein effect, combined with the influx of recession-proof City bankers with mind-boggling bonuses, had meant that across the county dilapidated barns and tiny former fishermen's cottages had been pimped up to unrecognisable standards. Cornwall's mild climate, Caribbean-style beaches (if you ignored the freezing water that turned unwetsuited bodies blue in minutes, obviously) and breathtaking beauty made it the number one desirable spot for second homes. In winter you only had to pop to Rock – that Mecca for the wealthy, with its chic bistros and fabulous property – to see the tumbleweed blowing down the main street and all the shops shut up until Easter. The Cornish couldn't afford Cornwall any more.

There was a tight knot in Gemma's throat. She was too late. The cottage had been bought by some rich couple from up country, and it would be Emma Bridgewatered and Cath Kidstoned before you could say shabby chic. The inside would be fashionably distressed – unlike the Lion Lodge, which was unfashionably distraught – and filled with bleached driftwood, stripped floorboards and calico sofas. There'd be a seaside theme too: maybe some blue and white stripy curtains, and on the white walls big splashy John Dyer prints of seagulls with yellow feet flying high above bright fishing boats. The spot where she and Cal had made love all afternoon would be long forgotten and buried under a kitchen floor of the finest Delabole slate, maybe with a bright rag rug laid over it for the obligatory chocolate Labrador to sprawl across. There would be an Aga too, no doubt: a giant cream affair shipped in as a fashion accessory rather than to cook on. Why cook when Truro had wonderful restaurants and Fowey was just a short boat trip away? Gemma didn't need to step out of the car and peek through the window; every second home she'd ever visited followed a variation on this theme, as city folk hired designers to create the perfect seaside getaway.

"Bollocks," said Angel, killing the engine. She put a hand on Gemma's shoulder and squeezed it kindly. "Looks like somebody had the same idea. You OK, babes?"

Gemma swallowed the lump in her throat. The truth was that she was absolutely devastated, which was ridiculous. The dream of her and Cal living happily ever after at Penmerryn Creek had only ever been that – a dream – and it made no sense that her eyes stung with tears.

"Yeah, I'm fine," she fibbed, and this time Angel didn't tease her because it was obvious that Gemma wasn't fine at all.

"It's a gorgeous spot," Angel said thoughtfully, winding down the car window and letting the sharp salty air lift her long blonde mane. "I can see why you like it so much."

Gemma nodded, still unable to find her voice, which she was sure would sound as cracked as her dreams. Angel was right: it was a gorgeous spot. Even on a December afternoon, with the light fading and the creek resembling a pewter-grey ribbon, the place was breathtaking. Oystercatchers waded in the mudflats, the blue flash of a kingfisher darted over the shallows and a beady-eyed robin in his Christmas sweater was chip-chipping away from his gatepost lookout. The jetty had been mended, she noticed with a pang, and a smart new

Boston Whaler boat was on a trailer alongside the house. There was an extension too, sympathetically done in matching granite and with a stylish glass roof ribbed with blonde beams, as well as a new stable-style door in the old pantry area. Whoever had done this had taste, Gemma thought grudgingly, and lots of money to burn too. Getting such quality materials sourced and then delivered this far off the beaten track wasn't cheap, and neither was the labour.

"Maybe I should have been a banker, not an actress?" she murmured.

"Not with your maths! Bloody hell, Gem! You read numbers back to front."

This was an unfortunate truth and it often made for huge disappointments on salary cheques and bank balances. Gemma was to finance what Kim Kardashian was to small bottoms. For this reason, and because she'd made several big errors with the business plan, Cal now handled the joint finances. There was a daily account which they both used for food and fuel, but she left the rest of it to him. Gemma sometimes worried that maybe this wasn't very feminist of her; however, they both had different strengths and it made sense to use them. Besides, since his horrific tax bill, caused by poor advice and a celebrity money-hiding scandal ("That's the fecking last time I take advice from famous comedians," Cal had said bitterly), Cal had employed Angel's sister Andi as his accountant. Andi was red hot; she never missed a trick, and Gemma trusted her entirely.

"It's called dyscalculia and it's a learning disability," she told Angel huffily, who just laughed.

"Call it what you like; I don't think Mark Carney's quaking in his boots that you're in the running to be the next Governor of the Bank of England. Not that I'm much better. If Stephen Hawking saw our overdraft he'd think he'd found another black hole."

No point asking if she and Cal could have central heating installed at the Lion Lodge then, thought Gemma bleakly. Thick socks and thermals it was. No wonder they rarely had sex. By the time the layers were off they'd completely forgotten what it was they were up to in the first place.

"Come on then," said Angel suddenly, unbuckling her seatbelt and opening the car door. "What are you waiting for?"

"What do you mean? Why are you getting out?" Gemma was confused.

"I haven't driven this far just to sit in the Land Rover." Angel was out of the vehicle now and striding towards the cottage, or striding as much as it was possible to stride in purple spiky-heeled ankle boots on muddy grass. "Come on," she called over her shoulder. "Let's check it out. You never know, it may still be for sale!"

Shoving the passenger door open, Gemma followed her friend up across the garden – although she really didn't see the point. Even if the house was being flipped around and put back onto the open market it would command a huge price and be way out of her league. The joy of it being a ruin had been that firstly she and Cal could afford it and secondly they could have fun doing it up together and putting their own touches onto it. Now the cottage belonged to somebody else and her dream of a future there with Cal was in pieces.

Gemma really hoped this wasn't an omen…

Angel, balancing precariously on a water butt, was now peering in through a window. One false-nailed hand clutched the lintel while the other fiddled with the latch; she looked like a well-dressed Goldilocks.

"What's that face for?" Angel asked when Gemma joined her.

"Angel, you can't go breaking in!" Gemma cast a nervous glance around the darkening garden.

"I'm not breaking in. I'm just having a look. Don't you want to know what it's like inside?"

"Not really," said Gemma. She liked the way she'd imagined the cottage. Why spoil that by hearing about designer furniture and the ubiquitous Farrow & Ball paint?

"Damn! There goes my nail! I thought I nearly had it then, too." Angel held up her hand and looked sorrowfully at her index finger, which seemed rather bald and stumpy compared to its fellows. "It's on the floor. Can you see if you can find it? I'll glue it back on when we're home."

And so it came to this, Gemma reflected, that she was scrabbling around in the mud looking for her best friend's acrylic nail, outside what had until minutes before been her dream cottage. Her own nails were soon covered in dirt and the knees of her jeans were grubby too. She sighed. There wasn't even the prospect of a hot bath to look forward to: the water at the Lion Lodge was a lukewarm trickle and turned glacial the second it splashed into the huge enamel bath. The bathroom itself was freezing as well, and although an asthmatic fan heater wheezed dusty puffs of air into the room, it made little difference. This had been fine in the spring when they'd first moved in. Buoyed up by the privacy and the sunshine streaming through the windows in golden ribbons, the lack of heating really hadn't seemed an issue. Fast-forward several months and it was a very different story. Lately, Cal and Gemma had taken to strip-washing by the fire with flannels and bowls of hot water, like something out of the Victorian era.

Cal had joked that they were only a step away from getting a tin bath. At least, Gemma hoped that was a joke.

She brushed the dirt from her trousers and sighed. It just went to show that there really was no such thing as a free house. No wonder Laurence had looked at them as though they were mad when they'd insisted on moving in.

"There's nothing to see anyway," Angel reported, derailing Gemma's train of thought. "It's totally empty inside: just bare walls and wires hanging out." She inspected her fingers again sadly. "Looks like I've sacrificed a nail for nothing. Give us a hand getting down, Gem. I don't want to trash any more."

It was just as Gemma was trying to help Angel down – the spike-heeled boots making it difficult for her friend to balance, and Angel's dress being rather too tight for parkour – that the front door of the house opened and a smartly dressed woman stepped onto the newly laid garden path. She was city-chic in a sharp black trouser suit and killer red heels, which were teamed beautifully with her short ebony bob and crimson mouth. A briefcase was held loosely in one hand and a large bunch of keys was suspended in the other. She was pausing to lock the house when she caught sight of Angel swaying drunkenly on top of the water butt. Her eyes widened.

"What the hell do you think you're doing?"

Gemma had a horrible sensation as though somebody had dropped a scoop of ice cream down her chest – a sensation totally at odds with the hot flush sweeping up her neck. She was just about to open her mouth and explain that this wasn't what it looked like when Angel overbalanced. The next thing Gemma knew, she was sprawled face first in the mud with her best friend on top of her. Winded, she closed her eyes and prayed that the kindly Cornish earth would swallow her up, right here and right now.

"There's my nail!" she heard Angel exclaim in delight. Eight and a half stone leapt off Gemma's back and, spitting out dirt and grass, Gemma was able to push herself up onto her hands and knees. A pair of bright red shoes, which were no doubt hugely expensive designer ones, stopped right in her line of vision.

"This is private property," said an unamused American voice. "You've got no right whatsoever to be here. You get me?"

Gemma looked up. The woman, tall and slim and in her mid thirties, was staring down at her. It was safe to say that the expression on her face was not welcoming. Gemma quailed. She "got it", all right. She opened her mouth to try to apologise, but this was easier said than done given that it was full of dirt.

Angel – who was already on her feet and still immaculate, thanks to landing on her best friend – was introducing herself as though at a garden party. "So sorry about that," she said brightly, going into her full-on, wide-eyed, warm-smile Charming mode. It had never been known to fail, and Gemma had seen it get her friend out of all kinds of situations. She wished she could bottle whatever it was that Angel had, so that she could sell it; she could buy and renovate a hundred cottages with the profits.

"How do you do? I'm Angel Elliott, Viscountess Kenniston," Angel continued, sounding like something from the BBC in the 1950s – although Gemma had a sinking suspicion that playing the archetypal Brit probably wasn't going to impress this particular American. With her lean figure and razored bob, she hardly looked the type to melt just because someone talked like Penelope Keith. Angel held out her hand. "That was so bad mannered of us!"

The woman didn't dispute this. Neither did she shake hands or acknowledge the title, which was unusual because in Gemma's experience people usually went crazy for it. Maybe that was a British thing and Americans didn't get titles – or real ones, anyway? After all, they'd had Lady Gaga for years. Instead, the woman glowered at Angel, who looked shocked by the failure of her charm offensive and the lack of recognition.

"This is private property," the woman repeated coldly, dropping her car keys into one of her tailored pockets and retrieving a phone from another. Her eyes flickered over Gemma, who by now was on her feet and trying not to get mud everywhere. The woman's thumb was poised above the keypad of her BlackBerry. "I ought to call the police."

"There's really no need," Gemma said quickly. The last thing she needed was PC Puckey turning up and then telling the whole village that Gemma Pengelley had turned into a burglar since she went up country. "Although if you did call the police," she continued, "the local bobby would know me anyway and be able to tell you I'm from this area. We really weren't up to anything sinister, I promise! It's just that I used to play here as a kid and I was really surprised to see that it's been renovated. We were only looking."

"Looking," repeated the woman. She seemed distinctly unimpressed. "And that gives you the right to trespass?"

"Actually," Angel said, recovered now and looking miffed, "in Britain we have the right to roam." She knew this for a fact; it drove Laurence mad to have ramblers traipsing through the estate, and he was always moaning about it both on and off camera.

"Not all over this goddamn cottage it doesn't," the woman shot back. She pinned Angel with a steely gaze. "And I don't think you have the right to climb on people's property and peer in their windows either, do you? That is, unless something very strange has happened since I graduated from law school?"

Law school? Of course, Gemma should have known. Only bankers and city lawyers could afford to buy the plum Cornish properties these days.

"I'm so sorry." Gemma was mortified. "We're leaving right now, aren't we Angel?"

But Angel, unperturbed that they might have a lawsuit slapped on them at any moment, didn't budge. "Is the cottage being put back on the market once it's finished?" she asked. "Only, my friend really loves it. Her partner's a Premier League footballer, you know. That's soccer to you, I think? Smaller balls and no padding and fit guys like David Beckham?"

The lawyer stared at her. She couldn't have looked more confused if Angel had started speaking in Swahili.

"You must have heard of David Beckham?" Angel was saying incredulously. "He was in the States for yonks! And his wife? She was Posh Spice. You had the Spice Girls, right? She's Posh Spice but she designs clothes now. They're amazing. I've got this dress of hers and it was worth every penny, even though my husband Laurence thinks it looks like it came from Topshop. I guess you guys all shop in Wal-Mart though?"

Angel was not doing US–Anglo relations any favours, Gemma thought despairingly.

"Come on, Angel; time we left," she said, grabbing her friend's arm.

But Angel shook her off. When the bit was between her whitened teeth there was no stopping her.

"Seriously, Gemma's boyfriend is a top footballer. He earns loads of money!"

Now, if this were true it would be great. Sadly it wasn't. Apart from being an ex-footballer with a greater passion for pizza than the pitch, scandal and lawsuits had claimed a huge chunk of Cal's cash. Angel's well-meaning hyperbole couldn't have been further off the mark. If Cal had been right up there with the likes of Beckham and Rooney for wads of cash, then would she really be washing from a bucket of kettle water when she got home that evening? The depressing truth was that although Cal had earned amazing money, he'd also been very good at spending it too. A combination of bad financial advice, too much booze, a very generous nature and a global recession had seen most of his wealth wiped out. Add to this his huge tax bill (which made Kerry Katona's look like a pocket-money sum) and a family who constantly bled him dry, and there you had it: one skint footballer.

Mrs Black Bob wasn't impressed anyway. "I'm afraid it doesn't matter who you are or how much money you have. This cottage has been sold and it's privately owned. Now, I'd really appreciate it if you could both vacate the property. If not, I will have no choice about pressing charges for trespass."

Neither Gemma nor Angel needed asking twice; this woman looked like she meant business. Moments later they were back in the car. As Angel floored the gas pedal – mud and gravel spinning as though the Defender was an F1 car – Gemma turned around in her seat and took her last look at Penmerryn. Dusk was falling now, and a small slice of moonlight silvered the creek. As the shadows thickened and the car headed up the hill, she watched the cottage and her dreams grow smaller and smaller before they finally vanished.

Chapter 6

The Lion Lodge was empty when Gemma and Angel arrived back in Devon. It wasn't the darkness of the house that told Gemma this – the wiring was old and often fused – but rather the knowledge that Cal was up at Kenniston filming this evening.

"Come and join in," Angel pleaded. "I promise we won't include any footage of you. It's going to be so much fun. Builder Craig is having his twenty-first birthday party and he's totally convinced that Kelly Brook is going to jump out of his cake."

In spite of her resolve to have nothing to do with reality TV ever again, Gemma couldn't help being intrigued. Builder Craig, recently signed model and hot telly totty, was vain enough to believe this. "And is she?"

Angel snorted. "Hardly! No, Elly from the village teashop is going to jump out of the cake. She really fancies him, *which you'd know if you watched the show,* and hopefully he'll be pleased. If not, it'll make good TV."

And this, Gemma reminded herself, was why she'd stepped away from being in *Bread and Butlers.* She was tired of having her life manipulated for the sake of ratings. She wondered when it was that she'd started feeling like this while her best friend became more and more obsessed with the show. Maybe she was boring? Or was it a turning-thirty thing? On Christmas Day, two weeks from now, it would be her big birthday. Surely she ought to be a little more excited?

"Come on, you'll have fun," urged Angel. "It'll do you good to come out for the evening, and God knows we need a laugh after meeting that miserable old boot earlier. Blimey, she was like a female Bond villain, wasn't she? Did you get a good look at her shoes while you were on the ground? Were there spikes in them?"

The memory of being covered in mud and caught red-handed trying to peer into the scary lawyer's house was one that would probably have Gemma in therapy for years. Apart from the fact that she'd made a total fool of herself, Gemma knew they'd been completely in the wrong and this made her feel hot all over. It was all water off a duck's back to Angel, though; she really didn't understand why Gemma was so upset. For Gemma, it was far too painful to share her shattered dreams, so instead she'd spent the journey back to Kenniston Hall working her way through a family-sized pack of peanut M&Ms while Angel sang along to ABBA's greatest hits. Now she felt not only miserable but sick too.

If there was a party mood, Gemma thought, then she was the antithesis of it.

"Look! The party's started," said Angel, pointing across the parkland to where Kenniston Hall was lit up like Oxford Street. "Come on, Gem. Cal will be thrilled to see you."

"I doubt it. He'll be far too busy working," Gemma said bitterly, and Angel frowned.

"Now I'm really worried. Babes, Cal adores you. Why on earth would you think anything else?"

Gemma shrugged. No sex? Cal working long hours? Never seeing one another? His mother always singing the praises of his sainted ex-girlfriend? Take your pick, she thought.

"Is it the no-sex thing?" Angel asked. "Because," she leaned behind her seat, rummaged around and then pulled out the lilac bag, "don't forget this! Honestly, Gem, once you've got this lot on there's no way he's going to say no! He's a man."

Flinging the bag at Gemma, Angel gave her a little shove.

"Go in, get yourself all moisturised and plucked and dressed up, light a few candles and I'll make sure Cal leaves early. And when you're grinning from ear to ear tomorrow don't think I won't say 'I told you so'!"

Gemma had learned a long time ago that arguing with Angel was pointless, so she took the bag, mumbled something and then stepped out onto the rutted track that masqueraded as Kenniston's drive. The reflection of the mansion's illuminated windows trembled in the black lake like a scene from *The Great Gatsby*, the party inside probably every bit as extravagant. Lady Daphne had mentioned riding her horse up the stairs but Laurence had vetoed this, details Gemma knew because Cal had retold the scene in such a way that they'd wept with laughter.

She tightened her grip on the carrier bag. See? They still had good times and the spark was still there between them; she knew it was. All she needed to do was to find a way of reigniting it.

As the taillights of Angel's car retreated up the drive, Gemma pushed the front door open and let herself into the hall. As usual Cal had forgotten to lock the door and for a moment she felt irritated before reminding herself that any self-respecting burglar would take one look at the threadbare carpets, the black mould and the sinister wallpaper swellings that brought to mind that classic scene in *Alien* and flee for the hills.

Sensible burglar.

Gemma dumped her bags at the bottom of the stairs and meandered along the dark passageway to the kitchen. The electricity circuit was working for once, and soon the kettle had boiled and Gemma was preparing a cup of tea and a hot-water bottle to take upstairs. For a moment she'd toyed with the idea of curling up on the big squashy sofa in the sitting room and turning on the Christmas-tree lights. The Lion Lodge was actually a very pretty house and the sitting room was her favourite spot, with its big fireplace, full-height sash windows and ceiling that reminded her of icing on a wedding cake. Last weekend Laurence had delivered an enormous tree cut from the estate, which had resulted in Gemma and Cal having a trolley dash through Homebase for decorations. As she'd lobbed in baubles and tinsel and strings of coloured lights, Gemma's imagination had been full of romantic images of her and Cal cosied up by the tree drinking mulled wine and stealing kisses in the glow of the fairy lights. Sadly a fantasy was what this had remained, because the sitting room with its high ceiling and rattling draughty windows was perishingly cold. Of course, there ought to have been a huge fire burning in the massive fireplace, but as neither Cal nor Gemma were big on chopping wood this was yet to happen. So the room remained cold – which was good news for the tree, but very bad news for romance.

Awkwardly clutching her tea and hot-water bottle, plus the shopping bag and a packet of chocolate digestives, Gemma headed upstairs for the bedroom where she and Cal tended to hole up in the style of two explorers in the Antarctic. Gemma switched on the trusty fan heater, picked up Cal's laptop and plucked *Fifty Shades* from the bag. Two big feather duvets topped their bed; lobbing the hot-water bottle in first, she dived into them, wincing as the cold bedding brushed her skin. Eventually, with the lamps on and her toes defrosting, and chomping on her fourth biscuit (Gemma figured that she was eating more these days because it was so bloody cold in the house), she flipped the laptop open. A bit of Facebooking was always amusing, but Gemma had a more serious purpose in mind: Cal's ancient computer tended to run very hot, and with it balanced on her knees she would have an extra layer of warmth.

Reaching for her fifth biscuit (which didn't really count because she wouldn't have any dinner), Gemma scrolled through her home page, liking a picture of Angel's sister Andi and her partner all glammed up for a charity ball, and then doing a quiz to find out which Muppet she was. Was Oscar the Grouch a worse result than Miss Piggy, she wondered? Fat or grumpy? Which was the bigger sin? Grumpy people could still fit into a size twelve, she supposed, whereas her waistbands were a little snug lately.

She reached for another biscuit. She'd get healthy again after Christmas and her birthday. There was no point before then, was there?

Having caught up with her friends, it was time for a bit of Facebook stalking. Gemma checked out the pages of several exes and a couple of girls she really hadn't liked at school before the mouse hovered over the link to another page. She knew that clicking on that particular person's page was emotional masochism but she found it impossible not to look. Like the biscuit eating, it was compulsive and very, very bad for her.

Aoife O'Shaughnessy

Click went Gemma's finger, and just like that she was plunged into another woman's life – and not any other woman either, but Cal's childhood sweetheart, the apple of his mammy's eye and, according to Moira South, *the one who got away*. Gemma knew that she shouldn't look, but when it came to the saintly Aoife she just couldn't help herself.

Back in the dark ages, at about the same time that St Patrick had driven snakes out of the Emerald Isle, Cal had dated the girl next door.

"Sure, and it was just a teenage fling," he always said to Gemma. "Haven't I dated loads of girls since, and don't I love you the best, me darlin'?"

He had certainly dated lots of girls – this came with being a footballer – but Gemma was (mostly) certain that he did love her the best. The problem was that Mammy South didn't. No, Mammy South, who was more terrifying than any comic creation Brendan O'Carroll could come up with, disapproved of Gemma with a capital D and in complete inverse proportion to her idolisation of Aoife.

Aoife was such a good Catholic; she went to Mass every week, she helped the poor and she said her rosary. You'd think she was on first-name terms with Pope Francis too, Gemma thought wryly, the way that Cal's mother went on. The daughter of the family from the next-door farm, Aoife had been an honorary part of the South family for years and everybody had thought – had *hoped*, Mammy South had sniffed, shooting Gemma a beady look from her curranty eyes – that one day she and Cal would get together. But for some mysterious reason this had never happened.

"Sure, and it wasn't so mysterious," Cal had told Gemma when she'd once asked him why. "Aoife went to Trinity to read law and I was shagging my way through all the WAGs. Anyway, me and Aoife? That's never going to happen."

"Why not?" Gemma had asked. "Apart from being with me, of course?"

Cal had shrugged and then given her a hug. "Aw, Gem, she's just not my type."

Gemma hadn't bought this. Aoife O'Shaughnessy was tall and slim with a cloud of ebony hair, eyes as green as Irish shamrocks and skin like milk. She also had a killer brain, great boobs and possibly even a halo too. And his mammy loved her – and Cal, like most men, revered his mother. It didn't make sense. Girls like Aoife were every man's type.

"Why not?" she'd pressed.

Cal had merely shaken his head. "Because she really isn't my type, Gem, and I'm pretty certain I'm not hers either. Aoife's just a good friend."

Just a good friend had slowly nibbled away at Gemma's peace of mind. Whenever they visited County Cork, Cal's mammy couldn't resist dropping in some little snippet about how Aoife had been home recently ("such a good child, Cal, she visits her poor mammy more than twice a year") or had been promoted or had split an atom during her lunch hour. OK, maybe not quite that, but you got the drift. It was as obvious as the giant picture of the Pope in the Souths' kitchen that Cal's mum wanted Aoife as her daughter-in-law and wished Gemma were on the moon. No matter how many times Cal reassured Gemma that he loved her and that there was nothing between him and Aoife O'Shaughnessy, Gemma couldn't help feeling insecure.

It was mad, she knew it was, but since when had jealousy ever been rational? That would have made Othello a very dull play. Realistically, Gemma knew that she *should* be jealous of some of the stunning models and actresses Cal had dated during the good old, bad old days of his Premier League glory. There was Laura Lake the pop princess – famous for her tiny shorts and suggestive dancing, which regularly sent the morality brigade into fits of outrage ("Sure, and didn't she have the smelliest feet?" said Cal) – or Fifi Royale ("Jaysus, she had more hair extensions than brain cells!"), both of whom were gorgeous with flat tummies and flicky hair. But Gemma never worried about them. Neither did it bother her when some kiss-and-tell slapper came out of the woodwork ("Feck, I probably did shag her, Gem – but, Jaysus, I was so off my face back then it could have been Sister fecking Wendy and I wouldn't have noticed"). Gemma was only human and she wasn't a fan of any of this. Still, she loved Cal and this meant accepting that his past was more chequered than a chessboard. Besides, she knew that what they had ran far deeper than the shallow trappings of fame or looks or whatever made great PR. Even more importantly, none of those girls could make a cream sponge to match Gemma's.

Aoife O'Shaughnessy, however, was in another league altogether. She was beautiful, intelligent, Irish and a Catholic; she shared Cal's history, she'd been his childhood sweetheart and, here was the crux of the problem, Mammy South had put her on a pedestal. What would happen if one day Cal realised that, much as he loved Gemma, she would never really be the good Irish colleen he needed?

Gemma sighed. She was being bloody ridiculous. Cal wasn't interested in Aoife. He'd told her that enough times, almost to the point of exasperation. She flicked through the Facebook pictures – for somebody so smart Aoife had rubbish security – hoping against hope that she'd see a picture of the gorgeous Irish girl with a man. There were always male friends but Gemma had yet to see Aoife snuggled up to somebody or, better still, snogging his face off. Gemma's page was crammed with images of her and Cal, although she had to admit that some of these were quite old. But maybe Aoife was far too professional for all that?

"Get a grip!" she told herself furiously. This was becoming an unhealthy obsession.

Leaving Facebook, she tried to distract herself with the property porn on Rightmove, but today cute cottages and converted barns weren't doing it for her. A few days ago she'd Googled a cottage outside Falmouth that she'd liked. Maybe she'd check it out again, now that the dream of Penmerryn Creek was over? The browser history should have saved it.

Hang on. That was odd. Apart from today's trawl round Facebook and Rightmove, the browser history was empty. Somebody had cleared it. An icy hand clenched Gemma's heart. She certainly hadn't deleted it, which meant only one thing: Cal had. She frowned. This was really odd. Why would Cal do that?

There's a rational explanation, she told herself while her brain went into overdrive imagining the very worst. Deep breath, Gemma! Breathe! Maybe he was looking at bloke stuff? Guys did that, didn't they? (And after all, hadn't she just taken a bestselling mummy porn novel upstairs with her?) Or maybe when the fuse blew the computer had reset itself somehow? She supposed that was possible. There was nothing sinister.

Hating herself but unable to stop, Gemma navigated to Cal's personal email, breathing a sigh of relief when she was able to get straight in. If there were any problems then she knew that he'd have changed the password. Feeling horribly guilty for spying on him, she closed the browser and shut the laptop hastily. Lord. What was getting into her? This lack of sex business was making her paranoid.

There was only one thing for it: she needed to change this situation – and change it soon, before she went mad. Maybe Angel had been onto something after all? Reaching into the lilac carrier bag, she removed the

Mrs Santa outfit, the handcuffs and the can of whipped cream that Angel had insisted she buy when they'd stopped at Bodmin Asda for fuel. Quite what that was for was anyone's guess. Finally, she drew out that iconic book with the innocent tie design and deceptively dull grey cover, and nervously flipped to the first page. There was no putting this off.

It was time to see whether Christian Grey had any good ideas.

Chapter 7

The slamming of the front door, followed by a loud thud and a shout of "Feck!", announced Cal's arrival home from the big house and roused Gemma from a doze. She hadn't meant to fall asleep – this was far too risky with all the tea lights and candles that she'd lit and placed in what was a hopefully romantic trail from the hall all the way up the stairs to the bedroom – but the sexy Mrs Santa costume was skimpy to say the least and she'd burrowed under the duvet to prevent hypothermia. *Fifty Shades* was all very well, but Ana and Christian's red room of pain was bound to have been centrally heated, and pneumonia wasn't sexy even if it was painful.

"Jaysus, don't tell me the lights have fused again?" she heard Cal grumble. "It's like living in a fecking Dickens novel!"

Charles Dickens was *not* the author she had in mind right now, Gemma thought with a little shiver of anticipation, although she did have *Great Expectations* for some *Hard Times*!

Earlier that evening she'd read a few chapters of *Fifty Shades,* before running a cold bath (which was probably a good thing) and shaving and scrubbing and exfoliating every inch of her body. Then she'd smothered herself in the dregs of her Coco Mademoiselle moisturiser before squeezing herself into the red and white mini dress and fur-trimmed hat. Golly, it was tight, and it the way it squeezed her boobs up and out made her look like a porno version of Nell Gwynne – but then maybe that was the point? It didn't entirely cover her bottom either; craning her neck to see her back view in the mirror Gemma noticed that it showed far too much cellulite for her liking. Maybe once

Cal clocked her boobs her wouldn't notice this? The candlelight should help too.

The thump of Cal's footfalls on the stairs galvanised her into action and, cranking up the fan heater, she fluffed out her blonde curls and arranged herself on the bed in what she hoped was a seductive manner. Whipped cream? Check. Handcuffs? Check. Edible body paint? Check. Gemma took a deep breath. This was it. Time to surprise her man.

"Miss Pengelley will see you now," she called huskily. Wow, with her acting background it was much easier than she thought to get into this role-play stuff. Maybe Angel was onto something?

"The lights downstairs are working, Gem. What's with the candles?" Cal strode into the room, flicking on the main light and instantly destroying her carefully thought out and flattering lighting. For a nanosecond he and Gemma blinked at each other, dazzled by the sudden glare of the one-hundred-watt bulb, before Cal started laughing.

"Sure, I knew it was cold here but I didn't know we were in the North Pole! Hello Santa! How the feck did you manage to get down the chimney?"

He couldn't have chosen a worse comment to make. With a howl of misery Gemma leapt off the bed, beyond caring now whether or not her wobbly bits were on show, and, slamming home the bolt, barricaded herself in the bathroom. Tears poured down her cheeks, ruining her carefully applied make-up and washing away one of the false eyelashes that she'd spent ages gluing into place. In the mirror a red-faced, red-suited figure in a too-tight cheap polyester frock stared back her, her silly hat flopping just like her hopes. God, no wonder he'd laughed. She looked an absolute state. It was a joke to even think she could pull this off. What would look sexy and cute on size-eight Angel only made Gemma, a size-fourteen girl with boobs and hips, resemble lumpy porridge poured into a dress.

Slamming down the toilet lid and collapsing onto it, Gemma buried her face in her hands. No wonder he didn't fancy her anymore. She was a joke.

"Aw, Gemma, will you come out?" Cal was saying through the crack in the door.

"You laughed at me," Gemma choked. She didn't think she'd ever felt so humiliated in her life, and as a girl who'd once modelled control pants this was saying something.

"I didn't mean to laugh, darlin'. You just took me by surprise. I was wondering if there were any little elves hiding in the wardrobe, so I was!"

Normally Cal's humour worked a treat when he'd been a typical bloke and done something wrong, but today Gemma was failing to see the funny side.

"You said I was fat!" she cried.

"I did not!" Cal said, sounding offended. "You're not fat. You're bloody gorgeous." This was followed by a hollow slapping sound, which Gemma knew was him walloping his own tummy. "I'm the one in the chub club."

"It's different: you're a guy and you look great and everyone fancies you," Gemma shot back. "Didn't *Cosmo* have you as one of their top-ten sexy TV chefs?"

He laughed that lovely dark-chocolate laugh that usually made her insides ripple. Today, though, her insides were a millpond. Cal was not getting away with this.

"Sure, and isn't that all bollocks, Gem?"

"So why say I'd never fit down the chimney?"

He bellowed with laughter. "Because it's capped, you eejit!"

Ah. Gemma hadn't thought of that.

"You've got to stop being so hard on yourself, Gem. You're gorgeous and I love you just the way you are," Cal continued. She heard his back slither down the door and his weight thump onto the floor. "Ouch. I must be getting old, so. I'll just sit here, so I will, until you come out. Only don't take too long; it's fecking freezing out here."

"I'm not coming out." Gemma figured that she had a loo, the fan heater and water in the bathroom. She could outlast Cal. He'd be an ice lolly in ten minutes.

"Ah, come on, Gem. I'll make it up to you." He paused and then started to laugh. "You can be Santa and I'll be Rudolph! I'll unwrap your presents!"

"That isn't funny at all!" Cal was lucky he was locked outside, because this quip had lit the touchpaper of Gemma's anger. "I was trying to do something nice! I was trying to act out a fantasy!"

"By dressing as Santa?" Cal sounded totally bemused by this. Although she couldn't see him, Gemma knew that he'd be tugging at his corkscrew curls anxiously. "Jaysus, Gemma, central heating and calorie-free cake are my fantasies these days."

"That's the point! We never seem to have time for each other anymore," Gemma sobbed. Both false eyelashes were gone now, sitting on the cracked lino like soggy spiders. "You're always busy working and I hardly see you."

"We see each other all the time. We live together," Cal protested.

He really didn't get it. Passing in the hallway or bumping into one another by the microwave did not count as *seeing each other*.

"Proper seeing each other," Gemma sniffled. She yanked off a length of loo roll and blew her nose loudly. Ouch. The cheap stuff was like sandpaper. If she kept this up for much longer she really would be Rudolph rather than Mrs Santa. "Like we used to." She swallowed back a sob. "Like when we went to Cornwall that time."

There was a brief silence and Gemma knew that Cal was remembering that perfect summer's afternoon at Penmerryn Creek. She couldn't see his face but she was certain he was smiling.

"Sure, and wasn't that a magical time?" he said softly. "The best time ever, but there are going to be more. So many more, I promise. Please come out, darlin'. I can't bear it when you're sad."

The loo roll was disintegrating in her hands and her bum was getting numb on the unforgiving toilet lid. Suddenly, being locked away from Cal didn't seem such a great idea.

"Listen, Gem," he was saying earnestly, "I know it's been flat out and I know that I've probably spent far too much time working, but believe me, darlin', I'm doing all this for us. Building the bakery and the brand is all part of the groundwork for our future. Even that daft TV show's just another step towards a better life for you and me. Sure, and wasn't it you who told me how much help the telly coverage would be for the business when we signed up for the first series?"

He was right. Gemma *had* been the driving force behind their signing with Seaside Rock, but this had been back when she'd still thought she wanted to be an actress and before she'd truly understood just how intrusive Cal's kind of fame could be. Nothing could ever prepare you for the devouring curiosity of the public or the exhaustion of always having to be on your guard. A fat day, a spot, an argument, a trip out without make-up – all these things were fodder for discussion or a story on a slow news day. Gemma still cringed when she recalled how she'd been papped pulling her skirt away from her knickers.

"I did try and warn you," he said gently. "Reality TV is not your friend, Gemma, and there's feck-all *real* about it either."

In fairness to Cal, he had tried to explain that a season of starring in reality TV could be very long indeed. It was acting without a script, he'd said, and Seaside Rock would want their money's worth. But Gemma – buoyed by Angel's enthusiasm and, she had to admit, tempted by the money – hadn't really listened.

"But you didn't have to sign for the second series," she said now, hating the whining note that was creeping into her voice. "You knew how I felt."

"I did, Gem," Cal insisted. He was starting to sound frustrated now. The ringlets would have been tugged into a crazy bird's nest. "I know it's been a mad rollercoaster of a journey, but I've loved every minute I've spent with you. Come on, we both knew this year was going to be insane, but it's going to put us in a much stronger position. All we have to do is just ride it out and I promise you that next year everything will be different. We've got to get to the New Year and I swear on my mammy's life and the holy cross that everything will make sense."

Cal adored Mammy South. He was also a good Catholic boy at heart and wouldn't make such a promise unless he really meant it.

"You really won't sign again in January?"

"I swear I won't," said Cal. "Cross my heart and hope to die. Sure, and it's nearly Christmas already, and then it's only a few days until the New Year. Bear with me, Gemma; we're almost there, so. This is my last ever brush with telly. After the first of January I promise that everything will look totally different. It'll be just you and me and the bread rolls!"

That was all Gemma needed to hear. She slid back the bolt from the door and tumbled into Cal's arms.

"You daft eejit," he whispered tenderly, putting his hands on either side of her face and rubbing his nose against hers. "Never hide away from me again, OK?"

Gemma, gazing into his big Malteser-brown eyes, felt her anger melt away like butter on a hot jacket potato.

"OK." She rubbed his nose right back and then Cal's arms were around her, pulling her tightly against his warm, cuddly body. She nestled into his chest, loving the way he felt so right, so safe and so utterly, utterly him. When he tilted her chin up and kissed her with his lovely smiley Cal mouth, everything was right with the world again.

"Now then, Santa," said Cal, a naughty twinkle in his eye as he beamed down at her. "I've been a very, very good boy all year! How about you let me unwrap my present?"

Maybe Angel was right about the costume thing after all, thought Gemma delightedly as, hand in hand, they headed for the bedroom. It was about time something more exciting than bread rose in the vicinity of her boyfriend! They dived under the duvets and kicked the hot-water bottle out of the way, and very soon baking was the last thing on Gemma's mind...

An hour or two later, just as the Kenniston clock was chiming midnight, Gemma lay on her back, arms stretched above her head and with an ear-to-ear grin. Even the mould blooming on the ceiling and the clouding of her breath couldn't dampen her good mood. Everything was wonderful! Nothing would go wrong now.

She should have tried this stuff years ago!

"I love you, Callum South," she said happily. "Come here and give me a hug.

"Sure, I love you too, Gem," he replied from the darkness, "and I'd love to give you a hug. There's just one teeny-weeny problem. Oh Jaysus! Ouch!"

Now Gemma noticed that the shape under the covers was twisting and turning and making the strangest rattling noise.

"I'm still handcuffed to the bed head," panted Cal, writhing like something from a Miley Cyrus video in his attempt to move. "Feck! I can't get free. Where's the key, Gem?"

Gemma switched on the bedside light. The sight of Cal wearing the fluffy Christmas handcuffs and her Santa hat would have been funny, but for one thing: the key to the cuffs was still in the lock and snapped in half.

Callum South, Premier League star and darling of reality TV, was well and truly handcuffed to the bed.

Chapter 8

One of the things that Gemma loved most about Cal – apart from the deep smile creases around his big brown eyes, the scattering of cinnamon freckles across his nose and his parmesan focaccia (which she really could eat until she was almost sick) – was his sense of humour. It was very rare that Cal wasn't laughing about something and he could generally be relied upon to find the good and the absurd in most situations. Granted, she hadn't really appreciated his jokes about Santa and chimneys, but that was to do with her own hang-ups. When he'd claimed that the handcuffs were still shut, her first reaction had been to giggle. It was only after electric light had flooded the room, and she'd seen for herself that for once Cal wasn't joking, that the smile had withered on her lips.

Cal, rattling his manacles in the style of Jacob Marley, and twisting frantically from side to side, was starting to look pained.

"Aw, feck! I'm getting cramp in my arms," he gasped. "Did you have to loop them quite so high over the bed frame?"

"You weren't complaining at the time," Gemma reminded him. In spite of this unfortunate situation her stomach did a delicious somersault. "In fact, I think that was actually your idea. What did you call it again? 'Bed knobs and broomsticks'?"

"Pull the duvet back up; I'm fecking freezing," pleaded Cal. He did look a bit blue and goosepimply, and he reminded her suddenly of the giant turkey her mother always cooked every Christmas. All Cal needed were a few stuffing balls and some pigs in blankets! Gemma couldn't help herself. She started to laugh.

"Aw, very funny, Gemma!" Cal wasn't looking amused, which was fair enough; after all, he was the one naked apart from a Santa hat, and handcuffed to the bed. "Come on, me darlin', get me out of these. Jaysus, it can't be too hard. They're only plastic, so. See if you can turn the bit of key that's left."

Gemma crawled across the mattress and peered at the lock. Bollocks. Sure enough, the key had snapped right inside the lock; a tiny splinter of plastic was all that remained of it. No matter how much she fiddled with it, she just couldn't get it to turn. Even attempting to pick it with a Kirby grip and tweezers failed miserably. That was her future career as a master criminal halted in its tracks – and Cal's career as anything but a fantasy Christmas-themed sex slave scuppered.

"It's not moving. What are we going to do?" she wailed, giving up and sitting back on her haunches.

"Panic?" suggested Cal. "Watch as the circulation stops in my limbs? Call the fire brigade?"

They stared at each other in horror. Across the park the Kenniston clock chimed a quarter past midnight and voices floated on the chilly north wind.

"That was a joke, by the way," he said quickly. "I'm not having all those hunky hero types pissing themselves when they see me like this."

"But shall I get help? Your wrists are turning blue." Gemma was really worried now. The cuffs had been a little snug but at the time that hadn't seemed to matter. Cal had even joked that he'd diet into them.

But her boyfriend looked mortified by the suggestion of her fetching help.

"No, no, it hasn't come to that yet! Look, maybe if I pull the cuffs against the bed frame then the plastic will snap?"

Gemma didn't hold out much hope, but anything was worth a try. She watched helplessly as Cal twisted his arms, frantically flipping backwards and forwards on the mattress like a landed mackerel in a scene that even E L James couldn't have imagined. Plastic clattered against metal and the bed shook, but the fun handcuffs remained intact.

"Are you sure you didn't get these from the local nick?" panted Cal. He sagged against the bed head, sweat gleaming on his brow. "Feck. What now?"

They paused for a minute to think, Cal with the duvet up to his nose and Gemma wrapped in her dressing gown.

"Maybe we could dismantle the bed?" Gemma suggested finally. "Perhaps the headboard will come apart?"

The Lion Lodge had last been furnished when Queen Victoria was in nappies, and Cal and Gemma's bed was an enormous metal-framed contraption – which had seemed a really great bonus ten minutes ago. Now, though, it wasn't quite so appealing. Victorians built everything to last, from bridges to viaducts to, as they now discovered, bed frames. No matter how Gemma tried to twist and turn the metal rails, they refused to budge. Cal was stuck.

Then a brilliant idea occurred to Gemma.

"Where's your toolkit?" she asked.

"My what?" said Cal. He was looking extremely uncomfortable and Gemma felt terrible. Typical Angel and her bright ideas. Next time if she wanted excitement at bedtime she'd just buy an electric blanket.

"Your toolkit," Gemma repeated. "You know, for doing DIY."

This was bound to hold the solution. Her father and brothers all had various kinds of toolkits and Gemma herself was pretty handy with a spanner. You didn't grow up on a farm without learning a few skills. Once she had her hands on a hacksaw Cal would be free in a jiffy.

"Gem, darlin'," said Cal, with a great deal of patience for a man who'd been chained to a bed frame for almost half an hour. "Have you ever seen me with a toolkit? When I have ever, in all the time you've known me, shown any desire to do some DIY? Sure, I might feel a total tool right now, but I do not have a toolkit. I'm a baker, not a builder. I leave all that stuff to all those muscle-bound guys at the Hall. If you want a toolkit then it's Craig you need."

Their eyes met suddenly.

"Are you thinking what I'm thinking?" said Gemma.

Cal paled, his stubble and freckles suddenly standing out like a rash. "Do you know, this isn't so bad. I'll stay like this until the morning, Gem, and then you can drive to Homebase and get us a hacksaw. It'll be fine."

His hands were blue and his wrists were starting to swell. He didn't look fine. He looked as though his circulation might be cut off at any minute. Never mind lasting until tomorrow when Gemma could go and find a saw; Cal might not last another ten minutes. There was only one solution and, much as Cal would hate it, they didn't have any choice.

She was going to have to call a builder…

"Blimey, mate! I never had you and your missus down as kinky! Like you're in your thirties, right? I didn't think people even had sex in their thirties!"

Builder Craig, fresh from his party and with several shandies under his belt, stopped dead in his tracks when he saw Cal's predicament. Two members of the *Bread and Butlers* crew armed with a boom mike and a camera almost crashed into Craig, and even Laurence Elliott was shocked out of his habitual aristocratic languor.

"Bloody hell, Cal!" Laurence's pewter-grey eyes were out on stalks. "Whatever happened to you?"

"Put it this way: I'm never letting Gemma go shopping with your wife again," said Cal. "Sure, I know you public school types get up to all sorts, but pain is not doing it for me."

Gemma felt dreadful. This was all her fault. She really should know better than to listen to Angel. She and Cal were more M&S than S&M, especially when it came to the food hall. Brioche and not bondage was what did it for them. Now, thanks to her, poor Cal was in agony and providing great footage for the show.

She clenched her fists so tightly that her nails dug into her palms. This was exactly what was starting to grate so much. Why was it that everything was always about the show? Laurence and Craig were supposed to be their friends and all she'd wanted was some help from them, or failing that a hacksaw. But as Cal had pointed out, reality TV was not her friend. When she'd called Angel, her pal had hooted with laughter before promising to send help.

"I just need a hacksaw," Gemma had explained, "to get through the chain. If Craig could drop one off that would be brilliant."

"No problem. He's right here; I'll send him to find one," Angel had promised. "See! Didn't I tell you buying those bits would make your love life more exciting?"

"This wasn't quite the kind of excitement I had in mind," Gemma had told her, but Angel had already gone, hopefully to sort out Cal's rescue. All things considered, it was the least she could do.

So when chirpy Craig had arrived on the doorstep at a quarter to one with Laurence and the film crew in tow, Gemma had nearly exploded. There was no way this was being filmed! When Craig had said he'd only free Cal if the cameras were involved, and Laurence had politely pointed out that Cal was under contract to allow filming of all areas of his life, Gemma had almost told her best friend's husband exactly where he could stick his contract. Only the fact that poor Cal was trapped upstairs, in pain and very fed up, stopped her.

"This will be brilliant material for the show before the Christmas special," she'd heard the producer say gleefully. "What a stroke of luck!"

Gritting her teeth so tightly that she'd half expected them to shatter, Gemma had let the crew in. She'd been ready to combust. Tonight was just the final straw for *Bread and Butlers*. Sod the contract. She and Cal were out of here.

Craig – dressed in a tight white tee shirt that showed off his sculpted torso, and jeans that were quite indecent around the crotch – was making a big show of freeing Cal, drawing the hacksaw backwards and forwards with excruciating slowness while making sure that the cameras were shooting his good side and that the lighting showed his rippling biceps to the best advantage. With his butterscotch tan, Armitage Shanks white teeth and flopping blond hair, he looked like he belonged to a boy band and had rolled up to shoot a video.

"I don't want to hurry you, so," Cal was saying, his face screwed up in pain, "but would you get a move on? I can't feel my fingers."

Craig flipped his hair. He was evidently conscious of the contrast between his gym-honed groomed self, the hero of the hour, and poor pale cuddly Cal who looked a total fool.

"I'm doing a good job," he pouted. "These things take time and skill."

Time and skill my arse, thought Gemma. Craig was so slow at his work a glacier could overtake him. He was hacking at the bed frame to milk the TV moment, rather than sawing through the chain, which would take seconds.

When he paused, wandering off to check the angle of the shot, she knew it was time to seize her moment. Wasn't there a scene a bit like this in *Titanic*?

"Do you trust me?" she asked Cal.

He gave her a watery grin. "Jaysus, after tonight? Never again!"

Gemma mimed at him to hold his hands out, stretching the links of the cuffs, before in three sharp motions she passed the hacksaw across the links and freed Cal – who slumped forward, rubbing his wrists and stretching his poor cramped limbs.

"And if so much as a frame of that is aired," she said to Laurence, "I'll sue Seaside Rock for every penny it has. Cal might be under contract but I'm not."

Laurence looked as though he was about to argue, but the expression on Gemma's face made him think better of it.

"We can still show the bits with me in them, can't we?" Craig was asking in a worried tone. "I thought some of that could be really good."

"Don't worry, Craig," Gemma said, shooing them all out of the room and down the stairs. "I'm sure they'll splice something together so that you look like a total hero as always."

"Eh?" said Craig, on whom sarcasm was completely wasted. Gemma gave up. She flung open the front door and ushered the crew and their disappointed star out into the cold night air. Actually, was it slightly warmer outside than indoors? Now that she was dressed once more in her customary three layers, Gemma found it hard to tell.

"Thanks a lot," she hissed at Laurence, who was the last to leave. "All we needed was a saw. You're supposed to be our friend."

Laurence Elliott ran a weary hand over his eyes. The skin was taut across his finely boned face and he'd lost weight, which made his hawk-like features even more pronounced than usual.

"I am your friend, Gemma," he said. Even his voice sounded tired. "But I'm also running a business here at Kenniston and the show is all part of it. Without the show there's not nearly as much publicity for Cal's bakery and certainly no money to pay Cal the Christmas bonus he thinks he needs. New ovens again, I suppose."

Gemma stared at him. "Cal wants a Christmas bonus for new ovens?"

If Cal wanted new ovens at Kenniston then was he thinking about staying put? Doing another year of the show? Surely not? He knew how she felt about that.

Laurence's expression was shuttered all of a sudden.

"Come on, Gemma, you know how the show works. It's our lives laid bare, no frills and no hiding. If we make the Christmas show a success then we'll all do very well; Cal knows that." There was a troubled look on his high-cheekboned face and his mouth was set in a grim line. "I can't say I'm a fan either but it's pulled us all back from the brink."

But Gemma shook her head. She felt exploited by this evening's events. Having the film crew in her bedroom made her feel grubby and tainted and utterly let down.

"You're wrong," she said slowly. "It's pushing us *over* the brink. Friends help each other, Laurence; they don't take advantage of one another. Just be sure to tell Angel that from me."

And with this parting shot she shut the door, leaving the Lord of the manor on the step, a bleak figure in his long waxed jacket and country boots. For a moment his lean form stayed put, a dark blur through the window panes, as though he wanted to come back and say something. Gemma waited. Was there going to be an apology?

A couple of minutes passed before Laurence shrugged and turned away. Apparently not then. Well fine, thought Gemma, at least they all knew where they stood.

Once the headlights of Laurence's Defender had swept away up the drive, Gemma braved the arctic kitchen and made two cups of tea and fetched the cake tin. She'd made a boiled fruitcake several days ago and it was one of Cal's favourites. She figured that after the traumas of this evening the least her boyfriend deserved was a slice of cake. As she cut him a thick wedge Gemma simmered with anger. How dare Seaside Rock use the events of this evening for the show? This was their personal life! And how could Angel have been so insensitive? Cal didn't deserve to be humiliated and portrayed as a laughing stock.

By the time she'd reached the bedroom Gemma had decided that first thing tomorrow morning she'd walk up to Kenniston Hall and have it out with Angel. They'd been friends for too long and been through too much to let this come between them, but Angel had to understand that she couldn't carry on behaving like this. Much as Gemma admired her best friend's ambition and all the hard work she was putting into turning around the fortunes of the big house, Angel had gone too far tonight.

"I've brought you some tea, babe," Gemma said, pushing open the door.

There was a low snore from the bed. Cal, worn out from a five a.m. start and the events of the evening, was fast asleep. He was buried so deep beneath the duvets that his golden curls, bright against the pillow, were just about all Gemma could see of him, and her heart twisted with love. If she and Cal could just be by themselves and away from the craziness of Kenniston Hall then everything would be fine; she just knew it.

Sliding in next to Cal, Gemma reached for the laptop again. Earlier on when she'd been in Cornwall she'd had the fleeting idea that maybe she and Cal could book another weekend away. Well, sod the weekend, thought Gemma, munching cake with great determination. They were going to go away for a bit longer than that. It was the least they deserved after this evening and working so hard.

Dream Cornish Cottages announced the website proudly. Now, as a Cornish woman born and bred, Gemma was torn when it came to the whole holiday-cottage debate. On the one hand she'd seen so many of her friends forced out of the villages they'd grown up in, as second homers pushed the prices of cottages higher than any local could ever hope to afford, but on the other hand she was now being seduced by images of log fires, snug sitting rooms and idyllic settings.

Seagull Cottage in Rock caught her eye instantly. Small, cosy and right in the heart of the pretty village where she and Cal had first bumped into each other (quite literally, in the doorway of a cake shop), it was simply perfect. A quick click through the website revealed a wood burner, a huge sleigh bed and a big roll-top bath.

This was perfect! She could see it now: her and Cal hand in hand strolling through Truro late-night shopping; having drinks with her friend Dee on Christmas Eve in a small Cornish pub, all low beams, real ale and swathes of greenery; and waking up in that big bed to unwrap their presents or, even better, each other.

For a second the mouse icon hovered over the bookings page before Gemma clicked. The next thing was to fetch her credit card. Stuff the show, stuff the business and stuff Kenniston Hall. It was time they put themselves first.

She and Cal were going to escape to Cornwall for Christmas.

Chapter 9

Gemma had no idea how she managed to sleep in until nearly half past ten the next morning – although staying up until three might have had something to do with it. By the time she'd managed to find her credit card, hidden by Cal in an attempt to stop them spending any more money until the overdraft was cleared, it had been almost half past two. Eventually, after ransacking the place, Gemma had found it inside the dusty grand piano in the drawing room that they never used. Elated, she'd booked Seagull Cottage straight away and then, carried away on a riptide of excitement, she'd ordered a deluxe food hamper, a Jo Malone goody basket and Christmas dinner at the St Moritz Hotel. She'd almost booked them into the spa too, but managed to restrain herself just in time; after all, they'd have the gorgeous roll-top bath to play with, wouldn't they? Once her Barclaycard had taken a serious hammering, Gemma had tucked it carefully back into the piano strings, returned upstairs and curled up next to Cal.

"Jaysus, you're cold," he'd muttered, pulling her close and wrapping his arms around her, which had been the last thing she'd remembered until the sun had crept under the curtains and tiptoed across her pillow. It was the unaccustomed sensation of warmth that woke Gemma. Stretching out her foot to locate Cal's whereabouts, she encountered only chilly sheets rather than the chunky hairy leg she was expecting.

Gemma opened her eyes and was shocked to see that it was daylight and that Cal, who generally started baking at half five, was long gone. A flask of tea, two halves of the handcuffs and a note on the bedside table were the only evidence that he'd ever been there at all. She scowled at the handcuffs as the events of the previous night came flooding back in all their humiliating glory. Then she remembered her Christmas surprise, which cheered her up hugely. Yawning, and hugging this lovely secret close to her heart, Gemma hauled herself into a sitting position and reached for the note.

Morning Santa! Didn't want to wake you – too scared what else you might have in mind! JOKE! Don't forget, birthday lunch for Daphne up at house. Drinks in library at half eleven. Xxx

"Feck," said Gemma. "Feck! Feck! Feckety-feck!"

She felt like the Hugh Grant character at the start of *Four Weddings and a Funeral*. How could she have forgotten that today was Lady Daphne's seventieth birthday lunch? Angel and Laurence had been planning it for months; all kinds of exciting guests had been invited and Gemma had been commissioned to make the cake. Lady Daphne, a law unto herself and one of Gemma's favourite people on the surface of the entire planet, had demanded a Victoria sponge with seventy candles, pink icing and hundreds and thousands. Laurence had been aghast.

"Ma, you can't have that!" he'd exclaimed when Lady Daphne had placed her order. "You've got all your guests coming; they'll be expecting something really spectacular!"

"Thanks," Gemma had said. She was off screen, so the cameras hadn't caught her flipping Laurence a V, but Angel saw and grinned.

"Don't be so rude, Loz. Everyone wants a Pengelley cake these days, and retro birthday cakes are fun. Maybe we could have jelly and ice cream too?"

"Oh yes!" Lady Daphne had nodded delightedly. "We must!"

"Sorry, Gemma," Laurence had apologised. He'd run a hand through his long treacle-coloured hair and looked increasingly worried as his mother had gone off on a tangent, planning sausages on sticks and cheese-and-pineapple hedgehogs. This was the antithesis of the sophisticated brand he was trying to build for Kenniston Hall. "But you know what I mean, Ma," he'd continued. "The Duchess of Ermingham and Lady Barrington-Smythe will expect something classic."

"Who says I'm inviting them?" Lady Daphne had said airily, and Laurence had looked shocked.

"But they're you're oldest friends! You were debs together and they were your bridesmaids."

"So maybe I'm a bit tired of them, darling? Susie Smyth is a dreadful bore – and Annabelle slept with your father. Although it saved me a job, I've never quite forgiven her."

This comment had quickly become an Internet sensation and one of the classic moments of *Bread and Butlers*. Laurence's eyes and mouth had been ovals of horror as his mother had then proceeded to not only air the family's dirty laundry in public but iron it too. Then she'd gone on to announce that rather than the genteel guest list that her son had envisaged, she was inviting the builders, her pals from the local pub, the neighbouring hell-raising rock star with whom Laurence was embroiled in a boundary dispute, and Cal's page-three-girl ex Fifi, to whom she'd taken a shine. After this, the choice of cake was immaterial. Gemma had slunk away at this point, nobody noticing her as Laurence and his mother hurled insults at each other. She'd soon been in the bakery deciding whether she needed to buy more hundreds and thousands to decorate the Victoria sponges.

The very same sponges she'd woken up at the crack of dawn to bake before she'd left for yesterday's book signing, and totally forgotten to ice…

"Feck!" Gemma leapt out of bed, frantically removing her tracksuit, socks and sweater and hurling them on the floor, and raced into the bathroom. One tepid shower later, she'd probably caught pneumonia but at least she was dressed and ready to head for the house. She had less than an hour to sprint up the drive, ice and decorate the cake and wrap Daphne's present (which was a *Star Trek* DVD – the original series, of course, because Daphne had a huge crush on William Shatner in his sixties' heyday). It seemed just about possible.

It was a beautiful December morning: the sun had remembered its purpose and was managing to cast some warmth onto the wintery countryside. Still, last night's heavy frost remained, and as she set off down the drive towards Kenniston (her poor Beetle was still stuck in the mud in Stag Wood), Gemma's Dubarry boots crunched on the iced mud and cracked the puddles. The lake glittered in the sunshine as though a thousand fireflies were dancing across it, and for once Gemma understood what Capability Brown had been thinking when he'd decided to place it there. It might make the Lion Lodge damp and add an extra twisty-turny five minutes' walk onto the journey to the house, but it also made a perfect mirror for Kenniston. The house's upside-down double shimmered in the water.

It was hard to be cross on such a glorious morning. Birds sang, mistletoe grew thickly on the summits of trees, and even her breath looked pretty as it rose into the blue sky. Gemma was still annoyed with Laurence and Angel – last night's misadventures made her hot with embarrassment even in these sub-zero temperatures – but she was starting to admit that there was a funny side too. Maybe once she and Cal were away from here and just on their own, they'd be able to laugh about it? Cal generally found the humour in any situation. She just needed to be a more like him and less uptight.

I never used to be uptight, Gemma thought as she reached the house and scooted around the back to the converted kitchen wing that now served as Cal's artisan bakery. Maybe it was yet another coming-up-to-thirty thing?

For once the bakery was quiet. The industrial dough mixer was whirring away to itself and the big bread oven was humming as loaves rose heavenwards. Only Daisy, Cal's apprentice from the local college, was present. She appeared to be hacking at a giant block of cheddar with a knife and stabbing bits of cheese onto cocktail sticks. Gemma liked Daisy, who was as fresh and perky as her namesake, and she gave her a wave.

"I can't stop," Daisy said breathlessly. "I'm making two hundred cheese-and-pineapple sticks and they have to be stuck in a melon and look like a hedgehog. And there are sixty party sausage rolls in the oven. Not made by us, either. These are from Iceland; she insisted."

"Crikey," said Gemma. So Lady D had plumped for the retro theme after all. She guessed this also meant that the mad rock star and Fifi Fluff-for-Brains were coming too. Angel would be thrilled. This would make great telly.

While Daisy carried on with her nineteen-seventies special, Gemma washed her hands, put on a white coat, hairnet and cap (the days of cooking in her own kitchen and sampling the mixture as she went along were long gone now that she and Cal had a registered business) and fetched the sponge cake, jam and cream and a bucket of icing. The sickly sweet smell made her feel a bit queasy and she was glad when the job was finished and the cake was there in all its glory, the edible pearl sprinkles glistening just as brightly as the frosty parkland outside. She was just trying to figure out the best way to cram seventy party candles onto the cake without razing one of Britain's greatest houses to the ground when a mobile phone began to ring.

"It's not mine!" Daisy said quickly. Phones were banned in the kitchen. The staff were in the kitchen to cook, Cal always said, not to take selfies with the first batch of the day. He was also paranoid about breaching Anton Yuri's terrifying contract, which gave Seaside Rock first dibs on any images to do with the business.

"Calm down. It's Cal's. Your boss has broken his own rules!" Gemma laughed. She'd recognise the Dukes Rangers' anthem anywhere now. Cal had actually been known to sing his old team's song in his sleep. Casting her eye around the room she spotted his coat hanging on the back of the door and, sure enough, when she slid her hand into the pocket, there was Cal's iPhone.

Funny. This wasn't a number stored on the phone or even one she recognised. It was a London number, she knew that much, but who would ring Cal from London? Everyone, bar the footballing mates he met up with sporadically to watch Dukes Rangers at their East London ground, was here. She could let it ring through to voicemail but some strange instinct was telling her to answer it instead.

Before she could stop herself, she pressed the green button.

"Cal, at last! I thought you would never answer. This is the third time I've called you! I got your message and I don't think she'll be a problem."

It was a woman's voice speaking – and not just any woman's voice, either. This was a lilting Irish voice which brought to mind the wide-open spaces, broad light and bright scrubbed skies of County Cork.

It was Aoife O'Shaughnessy.

For a moment Gemma couldn't speak: she was too shocked. It wasn't because Aoife was calling Cal. They were friends – she knew that. Rather, she was stunned that Cal hadn't saved Aoife's number to his personal contacts. That could only mean one thing: he didn't want anyone who might look at his mobile to see that she'd been calling him.

And by anyone, of course, that meant Gemma.

"Aoife, it's Gemma," she interrupted. "Cal's left his phone a work. Can I take a message?"

Or maybe even give you one, like get your hands off my man?

"Oh, hello there, Gemma. How are you doing?" Aoife said sounding generally thrilled to hear from her.

"I'm great," Gemma replied. Wow, it really was possible to sound fairly normal even when your teeth were gritted.

"That's grand, so," said Aoife pleasantly. Even though Gemma couldn't see her, she could imagine Aoife smiling her pretty little dimpled smile and twirling an ebony ringlet around her slender index finger. "No, there's no message. I just called Cal for a chat."

Gemma's eyebrows shot into her fringe. Had the sainted Aoife just told a barefaced lie? Only seconds earlier she'd said she was calling Cal back. And now it was just a social call? This had to be twenty Hail Marys and a few clicks of the rosary beads, surely?

"Are you sure, Aoife?" Gemma asked, so sweetly that it was amazing her teeth didn't crumble into stumps. "I'm happy to pass anything on to Cal." *In other words, we tell each other everything, bitch!*

"Totally. It was nothing important, sure, and I'll catch him another day. Take care of yourself, Gemma."

Aoife rang off, taking Gemma's peace of mind and the start of a good mood with her. Unease crawled along Gemma's spine. There was nothing solid she could put her finger on, but something was definitely afoot. While Daisy stabbed at the cheese-and-pineapple hedgehog, Gemma leaned on the window ledge and gazed thoughtfully out at the parkland. Two of Laurence's horses were cantering across the bottom paddock like medieval chargers, breath pluming from their nostrils, but Gemma was too lost in her own private misery to notice them. Instead the conversation with Aoife played over and over again in the sound booth of her brain.

"*I don't think she'll be a problem,*" Aoife had said. Who had she been referring to? Gemma wondered. Was it her? Would Gemma not be a problem because she would never notice that Cal was seeing someone else?

Wait! Seeing someone else… Seeing someone…

Hands shaking, Gemma unlocked the iPhone and seconds later she was scrolling through Cal's camera roll, searching for pictures from his last trip to London to watch the Dangers, as Dukes Rangers were fondly known, play. Surely there would be some pictures of the game? Or later on, of Cal and his teammates in the bar or at the Chiltern Firehouse drinking magnums of Bolly and doing whatever it was that loaded footballers did for fun? The trouble was that there were no pictures like this at all. In fact Cal only had a handful of images on the camera, and most of these were of loaves of bread. One was of Gemma.

Second to a loaf of bread. It was nice to know where she stood in the general scheme of things.

"Glacé-cherry eyes! Tra-da!" called Daisy excitedly, pointing to a cheese-and-pineapple hedgehog with demonic red eyes. It looked like the evil love child of Sonic and Hellboy. Daphne was going to adore it.

"It's brilliant," said Gemma, although she was now on Google and frantically searching for dates of the last few Dangers home games. Cal had been in London last week and two weeks before that; she remembered clearly because she'd been doing a book signing in Bath on one day and finishing a massive order for the wedding cake of the latest It girl on the other. The dates were easy to check, but since the Dukes Rangers website stated that the last three matches had been away games, it was pretty clear that wherever Cal had been in London it hadn't been at the football game as he'd claimed.

He'd lied to her, Gemma realised. Suddenly she knew exactly how the cheese-and-pineapple hedgehog must feel, because little darts of misery were piercing her heart as the thought went through her mind. Cal had lied to her. Whatever it was he'd been in London for, it hadn't had anything to do with football.

There was only one other explanation, wasn't there? Cal had been in London visiting his beautiful ex. He and Aoife were both lying about it, and you didn't need to be a genius to figure out why.

Chapter 10

It was just as well that Gemma had trained as an actress, otherwise there would have been no way that she could have carried on decorating the birthday cake and behaving as though everything was perfectly normal. Everything was clearly about as far from normal as it was possible to be – Cal was meeting up with his stunning ex, clearing his browser history and generally being secretive – but RADA would have been proud, because this was Gemma's finest performance yet. As she carried the cake, which was now bristling with candles, across the courtyard and into the Great Hall, nobody could have told from Gemma's sunny smile that she was crumbling inside. This was Oscar-worthy stuff.

It was all circumstantial evidence, Gemma tried to tell herself firmly. So Cal had chatted to Aoife and visited her in London? It didn't mean that he was having an affair with her, did it? There was probably a perfectly innocent explanation, although what that might be she had no idea. Besides, if it were so innocent then surely Cal would have mentioned it, not skulked around deleting emails and conveniently forgetting to add Aoife to his contacts book? He'd been behaving very oddly lately too: he was distracted and always wanting to work rather than spend time with her. Then, of course, there was the no-sex elephant in the room, trumpeting loudly and eating buns. It hardly needed the intellect of Sherlock Holmes to solve this mystery.

Cal must be having a fling with Aoife. It was the only logical explanation.

Wrestling with her misery, Gemma crossed the Great Hall, where pink lemonade was being poured and the TV crew was busy measuring the light and setting up the cameras. Cables and leads snaked across the floor and threatened to lasso Gemma's ankles. She clutched the cake tray tightly and prayed that she could get through the next couple of hours. It was only a birthday party, so just how hard could it be? There'd be plenty of time to speak to Cal afterwards, once they were alone and the cameras weren't rolling. Maybe there was a reasonable explanation? She certainly hoped so.

The library was one of Gemma's favourite rooms in Kenniston. The walls were lined from ceiling to floor with wonderful books, including priceless first editions – all of which were totally wasted on Angel, who despite her education and intelligence only ever read *Reveal* and *Closer* these days. The morning sun streamed through the huge windows; today the protective drapes were drawn back so that the portraits of past Elliotts, all with Laurence's grey eyes and sharp cheekbones, were beautifully illuminated and the wood panelling glowed like honey in the soft light. Gemma wasn't a huge fan of the portraits. As she set the cake out on the table at the far end of the room she thought that they all watched her rather haughtily, except for the last painting – of Angel, all blonde mane and creamy bosom – which beamed triumphantly out of its frame. Another person who'd let her down, Gemma reflected bleakly. They were starting to make a rather alarming list.

"Great cake! Ma Elliott will be thrilled!" Angel said admiringly, dancing into the library and looking amazing in a turquoise cocktail dress and sky-high Louboutins. The Elliotts seemed to be making money even if Cal wasn't, Gemma thought resentfully. Something was going wrong somewhere. Maybe he was spending all his money on Aoife? Perhaps she was set up in a stunning love nest in Chelsea or something? At the thought of this, Gemma's mouth went metallic with the urge to be sick. *She* wanted to be cosied up in a love nest with Cal.

"Are you OK?" Angel was asking, concern written all over her beautifully made-up face. "You've gone ever such a funny colour."

There was a whooshing sound in Gemma's ears and the room started to sway. She clutched at the table to steady herself as a wave of giddiness broke over her. See, this was what you got for missing breakfast. She'd always known it was a bad idea; no wonder all those thin actresses were always flaking out.

Angel put an arm around Gemma's shoulders and led her gently towards a window seat.

"You're working too hard," she said, settling Gemma onto a faded red velvet cushion. Then she grinned. "And I bet you didn't get much sleep last night either! See! I told you going into Pulse would liven things up in the bedroom!"

"Craig, Laurence and the *Bread and Butlers* crew weren't quite what I had in mind," Gemma replied. She took a couple of deep breaths. The room was steadying now, the waves of nausea receding. "Angel, how could you send them over like that? I was so embarrassed. You're meant to be my friend."

Angel looked down at the floor. She couldn't meet Gemma's eye – a sure indication that she knew she was in the wrong.

"I'm sorry, babes. I'm not proud of it but when you called we were in the middle of filming and Dwayne said that if Craig was going to lend his tools then it was going to be filmed."

Dwayne was the new producer of the show. He wore tight black clothes, gelled his dyed blond hair into lethal spikes and wore Gok Wan style glasses that Gemma strongly suspected contained plain glass. He really was that much of a poser and, being more ambitious than Macbeth, was determined to up and up the ratings until all the opposition was obliterated. Anton Yuri had poached him from another reality show, and shock tactics like today's eclectic mix of guests were his hallmark. Gemma hadn't been impressed so far. In her opinion Dwayne was lowering the tone of *Bread and Butlers*, and this was another reason why she was desperate for Cal to quit. Last night's antics had only confirmed her worst suspicions. This was supposed to be a reality version of *Downton Abbey*, not *The Girls of the Playboy Mansion*!

"You could have told Dwayne that this was a private matter," Gemma said coldly. "We're friends, Angel, and you exploited that for ratings. It's not on."

"I'm sorry, Gem, I really am." Angel's blue eyes shimmered with unshed tears, but Gemma was unmoved. Her best friend was so good at turning on the tap that she should work for the water board. "I know it wasn't fair but Dwayne insisted: no filming, no hacksaw. Our contracts have also got us by the short and curlies. All access to our lives, remember?"

"Not to *my* life," Gemma reminded her. She glanced over her shoulder and out across the park. The Lion Lodge, her break for freedom, was a small grey smudge on the far side of the lake – but it wasn't far enough.

"No, and I'm really sorry. I promise that if he ever tries to pull a stunt like that again I'll pick up the phone myself and tell Anton exactly what I think. Dwayne's an absolute bugger. He's been egging Daphne on for days, not that she needs encouraging. Did you know that Loz found her in the wine cellar yesterday with a load of her cronies from the local pub? They were drinking their way through the priceless wine that his great grandfather had laid down. Laurence was wild."

This was actually very amusing. Lady Daphne and her drinking buddies, a motley crew of retired folk from the neighbouring village, were hardly up there with Oliver Reed and Richard Burton when it came to hellraising. Gemma tried to smile but her mouth refused. How could she ever smile again if Cal was in love with somebody else?

Angel took Gemma's hand in hers. It had been tended to since yesterday's nail disaster at Penmerryn, Gemma noticed. Angel had an elegant French manicure this time, perfect for a viscountess about to host her mother-in-law's birthday party. "But it's not just about last night, is it Gem? You haven't been yourself for weeks. What's up?"

"I think Cal's having an affair."

The words fell like stones from Gemma's lips. She hadn't know she was going to say them, hadn't expected to say them, but now that they'd been uttered her fear was out in the world and real. It was no longer just a creeping sensation of dread but a solid and terrible possibility.

Angel stared at her for a second and then started to laugh. "Don't be ridiculous. Cal adores you! He'd never have an affair."

"Of course he would: he's a man," said Gemma bleakly. "Don't look at me like that, Angel. I'm not going mad. Call it female intuition if you like; I just know that something's wrong."

Angel pushed her hair behind her ears. "OK, I'm sorry if I didn't seem sympathetic, but Cal? I can't imagine it. What on earth makes you think so?"

Gemma took a deep, quavering breath. "I never see him; the not-very-much-sex thing; he'd cleared his browser history on the laptop;

there's never any money so maybe he's giving it to a mistress; he's lied about going to football matches in London when the Dangers are playing away; he's talking to Aoife on the phone–"

"Oh babes, not Aoife again!" Angel raised her eyes to the ornate plaster ceiling. "She's about as exciting as watching the grass grow. Please, get over that one. There is zero chemistry between her and Cal, I promise."

"So why is she calling him then?"

"Like, duh? Because they're friends?" Angel shook her blonde head. "Gems, I really think you're jumping to all the wrong conclusions here. There are loads of other explanations for all this. Maybe he was looking at porn on the Internet? Guys do, you know."

Gemma did know, but Cal was more likely to be found playing Candy Crush than surfing dodgy sites. Besides, sex seemed the furthest thing from his mind lately – more evidence, perhaps, that he was getting it elsewhere?

"What about the money then? The show is doing well and everyone else seems to be making shedloads." She pointed at Angel's shoes and raised an eyebrow.

"These old things?" Angel asked. "Vanya gave them to me in Rock. Anyway, you should know by now that all the money Laurence and I earn goes straight on fixing up Kenniston."

"So if there is money coming in, why are we so skint?"

"Huge tax bill? Cal's debts? His demanding Irish rellies? Setting up a business?" Angel ticked all of these off on her immaculate fingers. "There's nothing sinister going on there, babes. Besides, Andi's his accountant. Don't you think she'd say something if there was money being siphoned off for a love nest with Saint Aoife?"

Andi, Angel's sister, was as straight as a Roman road and made Carol Vorderman look rubbish at maths. If there were a discrepancy with Cal's finances then she'd have noticed straight away.

"Maybe she's bound under some kind of professional code not to say anything?"

"She's an accountant, not a priest!" Angel grinned. Then she gave Gemma a hug. "Come on, this is all in your head, I promise. These are just weird coincidences that you're reading far too much into. It's been a long year and we're all knackered. Just give it until the New Year, then everything will seem better."

"So Cal keeps telling me," Gemma said wearily. "Are you both in on some big secret I don't know about?"

"Ha! Ha! Of course not!" Angel protested rather too swiftly for Gemma's liking. "You'll be saying he's shagging *me* next! Seriously, Gemma, you've not got anything to worry about. Oh look! The guests are arriving. It's party time. We'd better get you a drink and then pop you out of shot somewhere."

And Angel was off across the library, a blur of blonde hair and red-soled shoes, leaving Gemma behind in her haste to join the party. Feeling as though she'd just been in a wind tunnel, Gemma pulled her ponytail tighter and smoothed the creases out of her skirt. Davey Davis, the aging seventies' rock star, had just arrived – and judging by the shrieking from Angel as he pinched her bum, he was in a lively mood. Lady Daphne was also in the room now, doing circuits on her Segway and cutting the corners dangerously close to the table and Gemma's cake. The film crew was trailing behind, and unless Gemma made a move she'd be in shot, which was not what she needed.

The party was about to get started, but before Gemma could relax there were seventy candles to light, sausage rolls to fetch and the Hellboy-meets-Sonic cheese-and-pineapple hedgehogs to place on the table as the pièce de résistance. Her worries about Cal would just have to wait. Besides, Angel was right. It was all just a load of strange coincidences.

So why then wouldn't that twisty feeling of unease go away?

Chapter 11

December usually begins with a deceptive air. There are days and days to go until Christmas actually arrives; there's no need to rush because there's plenty of time yet to do the Christmas shopping, and the chocolate advent calendar is still deliciously full. Then, around the sixth day, time suddenly decides to pull a moonie and accelerate – and before you know it there's under a week left to buy the presents, get the food in, post the cards and, in Gemma's case, tell your boyfriend that he's going to Cornwall for the festive season.

Gemma hadn't deliberately *not* told Cal about their Christmas escape to Seagull Cottage. Part of her was desperate to tell him, but another part loved the fact that she had this amazing surprise waiting for him. There never seemed to be the right time to tell him either, because Cal was working longer hours than ever at the bakery or being filmed at the house. They really were like ships that passed in the night, or rather in their case bakers who passed by the industrial sink. Since the disastrous night of the handcuffs neither Gemma nor Cal had had the energy or the inclination to do much more in bed than pull on their layers and shiver. As the temperatures plummeted across England the windows of the Lion Lodge froze on the inside and the idea of taking off clothes in bed seemed suicidal rather than sexy.

As far as Gemma knew there hadn't been any more calls from Aoife, although it was hard to tell because Cal normally had his phone with him, which made checking pretty difficult. She was constantly looking to see if the browser history had been erased, which it hadn't, and to her huge shame she even logged into his emails just in case. There was nothing more incriminating in Cal's inbox than an email from a Mr

Eduka Buboni from Gambia who needed to borrow his bank-account details to pay in an unexpected inheritance, and a couple of adverts for Viagra. Feeling hot-faced and guilty, Gemma had quit Hotmail, but not before she'd half convinced herself that if Cal had wanted to keep secrets he wouldn't have "Dangers" as his password. Besides, they were a couple and therefore shouldn't have secret passwords. If Cal were innocent then he'd surely be happy to let Gemma look at all his correspondence anyway.

So why then, if it's fine, said the little voice of conscience that liked to whisper in Gemma's ear at the least convenient times – usually when she was snooping round Cal's Facebook account in case Aoife had left a message for him – *don't you just ask him rather than skulking around?*

Gemma tended to try very hard to ignore the little voice of conscience. It could more accurately be called a big pain in the rear end, mostly because she knew that it was right. Nosing into her boyfriend's emails and texts and social media was really underhand stuff, and Gemma wasn't proud of herself. There had been absolutely nothing incriminating anywhere and it looked as though Angel had been right: Gemma had just been putting circumstantial evidence together and coming to some crazy conclusions. Yet although she could tell herself this all day long, it didn't seem to make the slightest bit of difference. She still had the oddest feeling that Cal was hiding something from her.

"You're being paranoid," was all Angel would say every time Gemma raised the topic. "Honestly, Gem, I don't know what your problem is. Cal isn't having an affair – well, not unless he's boffing a bread roll! He's never out of the bakery."

So her best friend thought she was mad. That really didn't help much. There was nobody else left to talk to. Andi was abroad with her partner and Dee would just say that Gemma needed to work on her honesty in relationships. And there was no way she dared broach the subject with Cal. He'd either be hurt beyond belief that she could think such a thing in the first place or – and this was even more unbearable – he'd tell her that yes, he was in love with Aoife. Just imagining this made Gemma want to drown herself in the ornamental lake, so God only knew how terrible the reality would be.

"It hasn't happened," she told herself furiously as she drove back after a final last-minute Christmas shopping trip to Exeter. "It's all in your head, Gemma, you idiot. Everything will be fine once you get to Cornwall!"

During the manic build-up to Christmas this was her one and only ray of light; once she and Cal were away from Kenniston and in the sanctuary of Seagull Cottage, Gemma knew they'd be able to talk. With any luck all the horrible fears that had been stalking her would vanish like mist in the sunshine and Cal would explain exactly why he'd been in London. It would all make sense, and away from the pressures of work and the cameras they'd be back to how they used to be. It was all going to be fine. Their Christmas escape was going to solve everything.

Whenever Gemma had a spare minute (which wasn't often because she was mostly flat out icing and dispatching Christmas cakes), she booted up their laptop and surfed the cottage's website, loving the beautifully shot pictures and spinning dreams of how wonderful their time away was going to be. Last night she'd teetered on the brink of telling Cal about the cottage, but then Dwayne had called – apparently Cal was needed to pre-record another piece for the title sequence – and the moment had been lost. Filming was intense in the run-up to Christmas, and Gemma had gritted her teeth rather than snatching the phone from Cal and telling Dwayne that it was nine at night and that he could stick his pre-recording somewhere dark and, no, she wasn't referring to Santa's chimney!

"Not long now," Gemma told herself, in what was supposed to be a soothing voice but sounded even to her own ears rather hysterical. "It's nearly Christmas."

She was almost back at Kenniston, and evening had fallen in earnest. On the radio John and Yoko were singing hopefully about war being over. Behind her, the boot of the Range Rover was filled with Christmas presents. Exeter had been rammed with shoppers in that last frenzy of panic buying, the kind where selection packs of random toiletries and eye shadows suddenly become irresistible and slipper socks sell by the hundreds. Gemma had scooted through the city as best she could with six bags looped around her wrists, and by the time she'd remembered her original intention to buy a dress for this evening's meal at the Hall, she'd been exhausted already. Being elbowed from all directions while she'd browsed in Next and Monsoon had been no fun at all – and when she'd found it a battle to tug up the zip on a size-fourteen dress, Gemma had felt ready to howl. She must have been helping herself to the icing and leftovers without realising it. So much for walking up and down the drive to Kenniston twice a day as part of her fitness regime. Pushed for time and unable to face the horror of trying anything else, Gemma had decided that the Elliotts would just have to put up with her coming for kitchen sups in her jeans. It wasn't as if anyone was filming her anyway.

She swung the Range Rover off the main road and down the narrow lane that led to the Lion Gate. The headlights lit up the road ahead but otherwise all was inky blackness. Several tiny cottages set back from the road twinkled with fairy lights and spilled their buttery warmth into the darkness. Gemma imagined the people inside, cuddled up on sofas together watching the news or maybe tucking their children up in bed, and a lump rose in her throat. These houses were warm and full of light and laughter, not like the freezing spaces and deadly silence of the Lion Lodge.

Driving past her house (Cal could help her unload later), Gemma decided that tonight was going to have to be the night that she told him about the Christmas surprise. Today was Saturday and they were due in Cornwall on Wednesday. Christmas Day was exactly a week away. She couldn't really keep it a secret for much longer, and packing without Cal noticing would be easier said than done seeing as he didn't have a vast array of clothes. Once Angel's Christmas supper was out the way and they were driving back to the lodge, she'd tell him. He'd be thrilled; she knew he would. Cal loved Cornwall just as much as she did.

Parking the car in the courtyard, Gemma let herself into Kenniston through the back door. Built on the same scale as Blenheim Palace, the place was vast; sometimes Gemma felt that she needed a satnav just to find her way around. Angel had pointed out that most of it was uninhabited and crumbling away, but even the parts where the Elliotts lived were bigger than most people's houses. Angel and Laurence occupied the West Wing and had been busy converting it into a comfortable apartment. It was this work that Builder Craig and his crew had been doing for months – when they weren't posing about with their shirts off, that was.

Tonight's supper was to celebrate the completion of the kitchen and the idea was that they would all be sitting at the table in the new kitchen in a very informal Nigella kind of way while Angel dished up food, which she claimed to have cooked herself. Since Angel could burn water, Gemma doubted this very much; she strongly suspected that Daisy and a couple of other apprentices from the bakery had been drafted in to help. It seemed like cheating to Gemma but, as Cal was always telling her, there was nothing real about reality TV.

Angel's kitchen was huge, double the size of most people's, and already it was full of beautifully dressed guests clutching glasses of wine and chatting. Helping herself to one, Gemma glanced around the room admiringly. Craig might be the Narcissus of the building world but he and his team had done a great job. From the glittery black slate worktops to the salvaged flagstone floor to the enormous kitchen island, the room was stunning. There was a huge Rayburn, a giant American-style fridge and a stainless steel Lacanche oven that looked fit for a restaurant. The irony was that all this would be totally lost on Angel, who lived on salad. Still, it looked nice – which Gemma guessed was the point, because it was to all intents and purposes a set for the show. Take the massive scrubbed pine table, for example, at the far side of the kitchen and set beneath the glass roof. That would easily accommodate fifteen people, all of whom could be filmed beautifully as they sat beneath the stars sipping their drinks, toying with their food and hopefully creating enough drama to keep the viewers hooked.

Well, not me, thought Gemma rebelliously. They'd just have to shoot around her.

"Gem! There you are, darlin'. I was starting to get worried." Cal slipped an arm around her waist and dropped a kiss onto the top of her head. He looked gorgeous in brown cords and a periwinkle-blue shirt that picked out the gold in his hair and the sprinkling of freckles across the bridge of his nose. The curls had grown much longer and now they brushed his shoulders, making him look like a sexy throwback to an eighties' rock band – and Gemma had always had a guilty thing for Jon Bon Jovi. She nestled into Cal, leaning her head against his shoulder. Just breathing in the closeness, the *Calness* of him, was the emotional equivalent of sinking into a hot bath. God, she was such a muppet sometimes. Cal was his usual sweet self. Of course nothing was going on.

"You didn't find anything to wear?" Angel was asking, rather unnecessarily, seeing as Gemma was still in her jeans and hoody. Angel, on the other hand, was looking stunning in a red shift dress with her hair piled up on her head in glossy ringlets. She sighed. "You are such a hopeless shopper, Gem. I knew I should have come with you."

"Sure, but weren't you far too busy cooking to go shopping?" said Cal, catching Gemma's eye and winking. "All this food must have taken ages to prepare."

"Oh yes, of course I was," replied Angel, who was completely shameless and hadn't a clue what they were about to eat. "I was flat out all afternoon err… chopping stuff up and boiling it and things."

"She's more full of the auld blarney than me," Cal whispered to Gemma as they took their seats at the enormous table. "Daisy and Adam have been busy all afternoon; she paid them a wad to do this. I had to draft a couple of the crew in to help me."

"If anyone can carry it off, Angel can," Gemma whispered back. "Look how she managed to convince half of Rock she was a millionaire's daughter while we were actually living in that tatty caravan."

Cal reached under the table and laced their fingers together. "I have some wonderful memories of that caravan, so I do. I won't hear a word against it."

Lost in some very happy memories, Gemma daydreamed most of her way through the mushroom-and-cognac pâté starter. It had been a long day – Exeter on the last Saturday before Christmas was not a destination for the fainthearted – and the hours of elbow wars and basket rage were starting to take their toll. By the time she was halfway through the steak stroganoff and a glass of red wine, Gemma's eyes were heavy. Conversations ebbed and flowed around her. Now and then there would be a ripple of laughter as Lady Daphne said something funny, or an outcry (such as when Craig tried to eat the bouquet garni and almost choked), but generally it was a relaxed and chilled evening. Cal's hand wandered up and down Gemma's jeaned leg quite a lot and she was almost hopeful that when they got back to the Lion Lodge he might cuddle something a little more exciting than the hot-water bottle. Even the film crew and Dwayne didn't seem as intrusive as usual.

Gemma swirled her Merlot happily. She ought to drink red wine more often if it made her feel this mellow.

It was only when she was halfway through her sticky-toffee pudding (sod it, she was already a fourteen, so she may as well enjoy herself and diet in the New Year) that Gemma tuned back into the conversation with a jolt. The topic of discussion had turned to Christmas and specifically the Christmas special. Not being a member of the *Bread and Butlers* cast, Gemma hadn't really paid much attention to this to date, but now her ears were out on elastic, especially as Cal was joining in.

"So we'll all eat in the Great Dining Room," Lady Daphne was saying. "We could eat naked like the Fifth Viscount did. That could be a hoot."

"Ma, we'd all die of cold," Laurence drawled. "Besides, I don't want to be put off my Christmas pud looking at everyone in the buff."

"Don't be such a prude, Laurence," said his mother mildly. "Your maternal grandmother served herself up naked for a hunting breakfast once, I'll have you know." Her eyes took on a faraway look. "Maybe I could do the same but with pigs in blankets and stuffing balls?"

Laurence choked on his pudding at this idea and Angel had to slap him on the back several times.

"I think us all eating starkers is a great idea," Craig said excitedly, as only a gym-honed exercise junkie would; everyone else was looking horrified.

"Well, you can count me out," Cal told Daphne, shovelling in his pudding with gusto. "I'll be eating Christmas dinner fully clothed, thanks. Sure, we don't want to scare the viewers and put them off their dinners."

What was this? Gemma could hardly believe her ears. Were they really discussing Christmas dinner as though they would all be together and, even worse, spend the time being filmed? Over her dead (un-food-covered) body!

"We won't be here anyway, Cal," she blurted out. "We're having Christmas together and on our own."

The chatter petered away. A spoon clattered against a bowl. The tick-tock of the massive station-style kitchen clock seemed twice as loud. All eyes were suddenly on Gemma. The red eye of the camera light was blinking her way too, until Dwayne motioned for the cameraman to switch the shot to Cal.

"Darlin', we're filming the live special on Christmas Day," he said gently. "I'll have to be here."

"It's going to be brilliant," Angel added. Her eyes shone like a religious zealot's. "*TOWIE* did a live show once, but ours is going to be a million times better. We've got so many fantastic ideas to play with." She paused, as if waiting for Gemma to slap herself on the forehead and say, *Oh yes, silly me; I'd forgotten*, and *Don't worry! We'll be here after all.* But that wasn't going to happen.

"Cal and I are having Christmas on our own," Gemma repeated. "We never get time together and it's my thirtieth birthday on Christmas Day too. We won't be here because–" She took a deep breath. This wasn't quite how she'd imagined telling Cal about Seagull Cottage, but it was time to come clean. "I've booked us a cottage in Cornwall, so we're going to be there. Sorry."

There. The secret was out at last. Gemma turned to Cal, waiting for him to say that it was a wonderful surprise, that he couldn't wait and, feck the show, he was going to spend Christmas with her.

Only Cal didn't do this. Rather than seeming overjoyed he looked utterly horrified. Gemma had a terrible cold sensation all over, like a hot flush in reverse. Oh God, it was the ultimate humiliation. Her boyfriend didn't want to go away with her. The thought appalled him.

Her instincts had been right all along. Cal was no longer in love with her.

Chapter 12

It was like one of those awful dreams when you're in the middle of the supermarket and suddenly realise that you're naked. Everyone is staring at you and all you want to do is run away and hide – but your legs can't move and so you remain rooted to the spot, wishing that you could drop through the floor. Actually, this was worse: even though she was fully dressed, Gemma felt that she'd been stripped bare in every other way. The cameras were still filming Cal's reaction and so far nobody else had dared to speak.

"Aw, feck, Gem," Cal said finally. The pudding spoon returned to his bowl, a sure sign if ever there was one that he was upset. "I had no idea you were planning this. I wish you'd said something."

He did? Gemma was actually wishing that she'd had her tongue removed at birth.

"It wouldn't have been much of a surprise then," she said bitterly. Or maybe shock? Call it what you will. Cal was hardly jumping for joy.

"The Christmas show will be lots of fun," Angel said helpfully. "You'll love it, Gemma, I promise. There are going to be loads of really cool guests."

Gemma ignored her. Sometimes Angel just didn't know when to let up. Quite frankly her best friend could have invited Brad Pitt and Johnny Depp for Christmas at Kenniston, stripped them naked and covered them in chocolate and Gemma couldn't have cared less. All she'd wanted was to spend Christmas and her special birthday somewhere quiet with the man she loved. They needed that break before being here broke them.

"We couldn't have gone anyway," Cal was saying. "My family's coming for Christmas, aren't they? Sure, they're really excited about it too. Especially Dougal!"

If there was ever a straw to break the camel's back, then this was it. The Souths were a noisy, scrapping bunch. The many times that they had been over – a brother or two at a time, or Mammy South and a couple of the sisters – were probably responsible for Gemma's first grey hairs. Dougal, at twenty the eldest of the brothers and hell on legs, was going to cause havoc. Throw the whole bunch of them into the mix and it would be mayhem. Which of course was exactly why they had been invited.

Gemma looked at Angel, who was suddenly studying the contents of her pudding bowl with great concentration.

"Isn't it strange that nobody thought to mention this to me?" Gemma said icily. Nobody could look her in the eye. Even Lady Daphne and Craig wore sheepish expressions. Great. Everybody had been in on this apart from her. Gemma's stomach lurched. What other secrets could they be keeping? Glancing around at all of them, she added, "Didn't you think I might notice nine Irish visitors rocking up to the Lion Lodge for Christmas?"

Angel's head whipped up. "They're going to stay here, Gem. It's not like we haven't got the space – and they've agreed to be filmed, too. It was supposed to be a surprise. You won't have to worry about a thing, honestly babes. It's all going to be taken care of."

"It'll be a great craic," Cal added hopefully. "A real family Christmas. Christmas is all about family, Gem, isn't it? We'll have plenty of time to go away later on."

"It's my thirtieth birthday," Gemma whispered. Even to her own ears her voice sounded tight and weird. "It's supposed to be special. I wanted to spend it with you."

"Darlin', can we talk about this later?" Beneath the table Cal was trying to reach for her hand but Gemma snatched it away. No amount of sweet-talking or handholding was going to get him out of this one.

"It's my birthday," Gemma said again. "I'm asking you to please come away for my birthday."

But she could see by the taut set of Cal's mouth that, birthday or not, he wasn't going to change his mind. For such a sweet and easygoing guy he also had a stubborn streak a mile wide.

"Sure, I'd love nothing more than Christmas somewhere quiet, but I can't just walk away," he said firmly. "First of all it's my family we're talking about and I won't let them down. Then there's the business to take care of, and on top of that there's also the show and the small matter of my contract. I have to be here, darlin'. I'm sorry but that's a fact."

"We'll do something here," Laurence said quickly. He was always the first to try to smooth things over or find a solution, but even the UN would have struggled to solve this one. "We'll throw you an amazing party."

"And as soon as the year is over you and I will go away," Cal promised. "How about that, darlin'?"

Gemma shrugged. What did it matter? Her lovely dream of a romantic Christmas was well and truly shattered. Cal had made it clear that she was right at the bottom of his list of priorities. A sob rose in her throat and, unable to bear the situation any longer, she pushed her seat away from the table and fled from the room.

"I think that's a 'no', mate," she heard Craig say.

And for once Craig was spot on.

"Gemma! Gemma!" Cal strode into the bakery, flicking on the huge fluorescent lights and flooding the place with a bright white glare. "Jaysus! What a fecking thing to spring on me! Can we at least talk about it like adults?"

Gemma had been sitting in the dark, trying to collect herself. As soon as she'd left Angel's kitchen she'd burst into a storm of weeping. Unlike some women who sobbed prettily, Gemma knew that she looked dreadful when she blubbed. By the time she'd crossed the courtyard it would be snot and a red nose and eyes resembling those on Daisy's much-celebrated cheese-and-pineapple hedgehogs. She'd thought about driving home in the Range Rover but she'd had several glasses of wine and was bound to end up in the lake. Walking all that way in her high-heeled boots hadn't appealed either, so instead she'd bolted for the bakery and howled for a bit in the darkness. Now as she blinked up at Cal in the unexpected stark light she was surprised to find that her misery had been swiftly usurped by fury.

"What a thing for *me* to spring on *you*? And just when were you going to let me know that the entire South clan was arriving here for Christmas? The day before? Or maybe you hoped I'd think that Santa had just dropped them down the chimney?"

"Don't be so fecking infantile!" Cal shook his head. "Gemma, I'm sorry I never mentioned it. To be honest Christmas couldn't be further from my mind right now. I've got a lot on, so."

He stopped abruptly.

"What?" demanded Gemma. "Don't stop now, Cal. What have you got on that's so important you forgot all about Christmas and my thirtieth birthday?"

"That's not fair. I've never forgotten about your birthday. I've been thinking about it loads," Cal said. He looked hurt. "Anyways, you were the one who said you didn't want to make a fuss. I thought we'd do something in the New Year."

Men! They really were from Mars – and to be honest, right now Gemma thought the world would be a far better place for womankind if they'd all bloody well stayed there too. Of course she'd said that she didn't want a fuss for her birthday, but she hadn't meant it, had she? Everybody knew that when a woman said she didn't want a fuss that she in fact wanted the exact opposite! The kind of fuss that made Louis XIV in his Versailles heyday look understated and some jewellery so blinging that even Snoop Dogg would wince. Gemma hated herself for it, but a huge part of her had been hoping that maybe, just maybe, Cal was planning to propose on her birthday. That would explain why he'd been so secretive lately, the chunk of money taken from their current account and even the mysterious trips to London.

How wrong could you get?

She wiped her eyes on her sleeve. "Cal, I really think we need some time out right now. I booked this gorgeous cottage for us to just spend some time together. It's in Rock too. We'll have such a wonderful time."

"Darlin', I don't doubt it. Believe me, I'd love to get away too, but I'm under contract until the end of the month. I can't just walk away. Jaysus, Anton Yuri will have a hit out on me if I walk."

"Don't use Anton Yuri as an excuse. If you wanted to go away then you would," Gemma said bitterly. "You love that bloody show and the fame more than you love me."

Cal stared at her, his face bleak in the harsh lighting. "It's nice to know what you really think of me. Can I just remind you for a fecking minute who it was who wanted to do this show in the first place? You, I seem to remember, Gemma – not me. I told you I was sick to the back teeth of reality shows and fame. Sure, it's all bollocks. But you thought it was a good idea so I went along with it for you. It was the right thing, as it turned out, and all along I thought I was doing this for us. For our future."

"We won't have a future if it carries on like this!" Gemma exclaimed. Bugger, she was crying again, big splashy tears that were plopping onto the spotless floor. "Please Cal, can't you speak to Laurence? See if he can get you out of the Christmas show?"

"Gem, how can I? We made a commitment to Seaside Rock. You may not be under contract anymore, but I've made a commitment – and I'd hope you know me well enough now to know I don't break my word or lie."

"Yeah, right. Like when you said you were in London at a Dangers game when they were playing at Old Trafford?" As soon as she'd hurled these words at Cal Gemma would have given anything to snatch them back, but that was impossible. She'd opened the lid on her personal Pandora's Box now, and there was no reclosing it.

"You've been checking up on me?" Cal ran a hand through his curls, making them stand on end in outrage. "Jaysus, Gemma. What the feck is going on with you?"

"What's going on with *me?* That's rich coming from the man who's taking secret calls from his ex and who clears the web-browser history! Don't look so surprised! I'm just not as stupid as you think I am. And I wasn't checking up on you either. A call came through to your phone and – surprise, surprise – it was bloody Aoife. Don't tell me; she's coming for Christmas too, is she?"

"Bloody hell, Gemma!" Cal was staring at her in horror. "Is that really what you think of me? Do you really think I'm the sort of man who'd treat you like that?"

Gemma looked away, unable to bear seeing the hurt on his face.

"I don't know anymore," she whispered. "I'm so confused. We never spend time together, you're so secretive and then Aoife's phoning."

Cal raised his eyes to the strip lights. "Aw, feck it, Gemma! Not this again. How many times do I have to tell you? There is nothing going on between me and Aoife! There never really was and I can promise you one hundred percent that there never will be. You're being fecking ridiculous."

"Thanks for the vote of confidence," Gemma said sarcastically. "It's nice to know you're taking my feelings seriously. Why were you in London again?"

Cal exhaled gustily. "Sure, and can't you just trust me? Look, Gemma, just give me until the New Year. I can't change my contract this late in the day and I'm not going to let the others down either. Let's get Christmas over and done with and once my contract finishes on the first we'll celebrate without a load of cameras up our arses."

"You're asking me to postpone Christmas and my birthday until a stupid reality-TV show is over?" Gemma couldn't believe it. Just how insensitive could a man be?

"Surely it isn't the dates that matter but that we're together?" said Cal softly. "And that I love you more than anything? Even soda bread and Irish butter?"

He held out his arms to her, and for a second Gemma wavered. She wanted nothing more than to say *yes* and throw herself into Cal's embrace, bury her face in his chest and feel his heart beating against her cheek, but there were still far too many questions left unanswered. He was keeping something from her.

"Can't you tell me what you were doing in London?" she said.

A shuttered expression came over Cal's face and his arms fell to his side.

"If you can't trust me when I say that I wasn't there to cheat on you with Aoife, then I'm not sure I know where we're going," he said. "Jaysus, Gemma, just trust me. Let me get Christmas out the way and then I swear on my mammy's life everything will be good again; better than good."

"So that's it? You're still going to spend Christmas at Kenniston?" Gemma responded incredulously. "After everything I've said?"

Cal nodded. His eyes locked with hers. "I won't break my word, Gemma, not even for you."

There was a knot tightening in Gemma's throat. "Fine. I hope you enjoy it, because I won't be there. I'm not tied into any stupid contract. I'll have Christmas, and my birthday, on my own."

"You're being really unfair," said Cal. "All I'm asking for is a fortnight. After that, I promise, it's just you and me. It'll be grand."

"And all I'm asking is that you put me first," Gemma shot back. "I think that would be grand."

It was stalemate. They stared miserably at each other, neither prepared to back down. Then Cal sighed.

"I'm going back. There's filming to do, so."

The air snapped and crackled with words unsaid. Cal smiled sadly then turned and pushed the door open, leaving Gemma all alone in the bakery with their ugly words echoing through her mind. It was the first fight they'd ever had where they hadn't been able to resolve matters with a kiss and a joke. As she mopped her eyes with kitchen towel, Gemma just couldn't believe that Cal would put the show above her. She had a horrible feeling that this was something that couldn't be put right.

She crossed the kitchen and opened up her fridge. At the bottom was a giant bar of chocolate, supposedly for adding into butter icing. Well, not anymore. Men might let you down, Gemma thought sadly as she broke off a chunk, but at least Dairy Milk had yet to fail her.

Chapter 13

If rowing with Cal and then eating her way through the rest of her chocolate advent calendar hadn't been miserable enough, the next two days spent circling each other and speaking with icy politeness were even worse. Cal wasn't going to back down and Gemma, who felt that she was totally in the right, had no intention of changing her mind either.

No, as far as Gemma was concerned it was a simple choice: Cal either wanted to spend Christmas with her or he didn't. He could dress it up any way he liked and make all the excuses under the sun. Gemma knew the truth. If he'd really wanted to spend Christmas with her then Cal would have phoned Anton Yuri and pleaded his case. Nothing was impossible. The simple and very painful truth was that Cal preferred to be with his family and at Kenniston than with her in a romantic Cornish cottage. Well, fine. He could spend Christmas with them and she would take herself somewhere else. Gemma was sick of being at the bottom of Cal's list of priorities, and if she heard the words "under contract" one more time, she'd scream.

Since their big argument on the night of the supper party, Cal had tried hard to persuade Gemma that if she would only wait until after Christmas everything would be fine. Quite how this was going to happen he didn't clarify, but he was adamant that things really were going to change. Gemma didn't believe him and, after several attempts, Cal had given up trying to convince her. The sadness in his eyes broke her heart and she missed snuggling up with him and chatting together about anything and everything more than she could ever say, but Gemma knew she had to make a stand. If she didn't then this would be the pattern for the rest of her life – and she knew that she couldn't live like that. Feeling that you were right at the bottom of the heap all the time was not very nice.

"You're being really unfair," Angel had kept saying earlier on that day. She'd seemed determined to plead Cal's case, which had started to grate with Gemma – and she'd also kept swiping icing from the bowl, which was unhygienic and even more irritating.

"Cal's only doing this for you and him," she'd added, licking icing from her fingers. "Mmm. Sod the diet; this is yum!"

"So he keeps saying, but he never quite manages to explain how. Take your fingers away from that bowl!" Gemma had shot back, whacking Angel's knuckles with her wooden spoon. "Missing my birthday and cancelling Christmas is a bloody funny way to show he cares. Besides, I've got a bone to pick with you too, since you conveniently forgot to tell me the Souths were coming for Christmas."

"I wanted to tell you but I knew you'd go mental," Angel had muttered sulkily. "And I was right, wasn't I? You're so moody lately, Gem. It's like you've got PMT on steroids."

Gemma had chosen to ignore this comment. If she was moody then it was with bloody good reason!

"Don't give me that. You know Mammy South is good for the ratings and you didn't want me to put the kibosh on it, more like," she'd retorted instead, and Angel had looked genuinely hurt.

"I'd never think like that, Gem! I only want you to be happy. Maybe Cal's invited his family here for a reason?"

"He really wants to ruin our Christmas?"

Angel had stared at her. "Since when did you get so cynical?"

Gemma had shrugged. "Since Cal decided to put *Bread and* bloody *Butlers* before everything and everyone else?"

"You're not being fair," Angel had said again. Gemma had pulled a face. Best friends were supposed to join in when a bit of boyfriend-bashing was in order, not take their sides. Honestly, it was bizarre how Angel was suddenly Cal's biggest fan. At this rate she'd soon be wearing a Team Cal tee shirt. Gemma supposed it was a *Bread and Butlers* loyalty thing. Well, fine. Let Angel be on Cal's side if she wanted. Gemma wasn't particularly pleased with her best friend either.

Angel had flounced off in high dudgeon at this point. For a second Gemma had felt a tiny prickle of guilt that maybe she was being a bit hard on Cal. After all, he was a real family man – this was one of the many things she loved about him – and Christmas was all about families. But then she'd remembered that Cal still hadn't explained what he'd been doing in London or why Aoife had been calling. No, he was well and truly in the wrong.

So the weekend had limped by in a stalemate, with neither her boyfriend nor her best friend talking to her. Luckily Cal had been filming for most of it, so Gemma had buried her misery in finishing off work on the two elaborate Christmas cakes that her friend Dee from Rock had commissioned for wealthy customers. This was the time of year when Cornish villages came back to life as the second-homers drove down from London in their big four-by-fours, their boots crammed with gift hampers from Fortnum's, and opened up their cottages for the festive season. Harbourside houses, shuttered and dark since September, spilled light into the darkness once more and boasted huge Christmas trees and swathes of fairy lights. The locals galvanised themselves for a few frenetic weeks of action and opened up their shops, switched the ovens on in the restaurants and stoked up the log fires in the pubs so that Barbour-socked feet could toast in front of them. For a couple of weeks the county would buzz, before the New Year arrived and the holidaying crowds returned to their merchant banks and private schools. Dee, who ran the local bakery Rock Cakes, was practically rubbing her hands together when Christmas arrived – and the mini season was good news for Gemma too, because it brought in extra orders for Pengelleys.

Today was a glacial December Monday, so cold that Craig and his builder crew were actually wearing sweaters and hats as they toiled high up on the Kenniston roof, and the parkland was iced with a heavy hoar frost, making it look just like one of Gemma's Christmas cakes, complete with wide-eyed fallow deer and plump red-breasted robins. It was mid morning and Gemma and Cal were both in the Kenniston bakery, studiously ignoring one another as they worked, when Dwayne the producer strutted in.

Cal looked up from the Parmesan and cherry-tomato bread he was painstakingly hand glazing, and a frown dipped between his brows. He hated being interrupted when he was working and the all-access contract was a constant source of irritation to him. *Good*, Gemma found herself thinking nastily. *I hope you get as fed up with it as I am!*

"I've finished going through the edits for the Christmas Eve episode," Dwayne announced to Cal, ignoring Gemma as usual; since she wasn't in the show, she was of zero interest to him. "Angel wants you to come and view the footage before we link it to the network."

"For feck's sake, can't you see I'm working?" Cal barked. His hand slipped and golden egg yolk sloshed across the work surface. "Jaysus, that's great." Turning to Dwayne, he said, "I'm sure it's grand. Just send it."

"Fine," said Dwayne. He ticked something off on his clipboard with the flashy Montblanc pen he loved to brandish like Harry Potter's wand. There was a triumphant sneer on his face, or maybe he always looked like that? Gemma generally tried to steer clear of Dwayne. He might have done wonders for the viewing figures – great news for the cast, who were on a ratings-related pay scheme – but this didn't make him a particularly nice human being.

"Now, about the live Christmas episode," he began.

Cal shot a nervous look at Gemma. Honestly, what did he think she was going to do? Beat Dwayne to death with her wooden spoon for mentioning the dreaded C word? One look at Cal's worried face suggested that this was *exactly* what he thought. She had been a bit emotional lately. "Like PMT on steroids" was how Angel had put it, which felt about right.

"It all sounds grand, but can we talk about it later?" he said quickly. "I need to get on with these. The delivery van arrives soon."

Before Dwayne could delay Cal any further, a minibus taxi scrunched over the gravel and pulled up outside the bakery. The doors flew open and out poured a tangle of suitcases, arms, legs, snub-nosed smiling faces, wild blond and copper curls and language that would make Gordon Ramsay wince. Then the doors slammed shut again and the taxi practically wheel-spun out of the courtyard, the traumatised driver heading back to the nearest town and safety.

Gemma's heart plopped into her Uggs. The South clan had arrived for Christmas.

"Ah Dougal, ya fecker! You trod on my toes, so!"

"Mam! Mam! Did you hear that? Our Aisling just said 'fecker'!"

"Stop telling tales, you little shit!"

Thump. Bash. Shriek. Wail.

"Dougal! Aisling! Stop your noise now, or I'll brain the pair of you, God help me I will!" roared a voice that could crack rock. A large woman with Cal's hair and stocky frame lumbered towards the squabbling pair and dealt them both glares that stopped them in their tracks. Bright boot-button eyes swept Kenniston in the style of Robocop assessing a crime scene, and her lips pursed like a cat's bum.

"Now where's that brother of yours? Cal! Cal!"

At this hollering the pigeons in Stag Wood took instant flight and were soon half a mile away. Gemma didn't blame them at all; Cal's mother had exactly the same effect on her.

Dwayne was clasping his hands. He looked as though he'd just found the Holy Grail – and in reality-TV terms he probably had, because this lot made the Osbournes look shy and retiring.

Cal glanced at her, stricken. "Feck! I didn't think they were due until this evening. This focaccia's not finished yet and I've still got to prove the next lot of dough."

Outside, one of the little Souths was already shinning up the scaffolding like a monkey, while one of the sisters stared open-mouthed at Craig. Dwayne's eyes were as large as saucers.

"Fergus! Will you get down from there!" boomed Mammy South. She was marching towards the bakery now, a woman on a mission, and poor Cal was frozen. Quietly untying his apron and tugging the cap from his curly head, Gemma took pity on him. She might be annoyed with Cal right now but she knew how much his family meant to him.

"Go on," she said, giving him a gentle shove, "I'll finish up here."

"Really?" Cal looked so surprised that it gave Gemma a real jolt. Perhaps she was being unreasonable?

"Really. Go on, quickly! Before she comes in here and starts telling us we're doing it all wrong and only Granny South, God rest her soul and ten Hail Marys, could have made anything like decent soda bread!"

They looked at each other and started to laugh.

"Sure, and that's a grand accent you have," grinned Cal. "Thanks, Gem. Look, I know things aren't right at the moment, and I will make it up to you, I promise."

"Never mind that now," said Gemma.

Cal hesitated, torn between wanting to race outside and join in the chaos and saying something. The need to talk won.

"Can we try and pretend that it's all grand? Just while me mammy's here?"

She bit her lip. "Lie, you mean?"

"Ah, Gem, not lie, just act a wee bit? I keep telling you, give me until the New Year and it'll all be grand. Try and bear with my mammy; she means well."

To Gemma this was a bit like saying the Germans meant well when they invaded Poland. Mammy South did not mean well and she wouldn't be happy until Cal had put a ring on Aoife's slender finger; of that Gemma was certain. Still, there was no point going into all this now – and certainly not while Dwayne was there, with his ears flapping.

"I'll be nice to your mum, don't worry," she promised, crossing her fingers behind her back. "The rest we'll talk about when we're back home and on our own. Now go and say hello and leave all this to me."

Gemma would have said anything at this point. She just wanted Cal out before – oh. Too late. Mammy South was in the bakery now and it was full steam ahead towards her firstborn. Seconds later she was clutching Cal to her enormous bosom and weeping noisily.

"My boy, my boy! Let me look at you, my darlin'." She stepped back and observed Cal critically through narrowed beady eyes, tutting as she turned him left and right like a jeweller assessing a precious stone. "You're looking pale," she declared. "You're working too hard, my boy."

"Aw, Mammy, you know how it is, so," said Cal, and Gemma rolled her eyes. Here we go, she thought despairingly; time for her sexy, gorgeous, successful man to regress to a twelve-year-old. He'd be climbing on her lap in a minute.

"And you've lost weight, so you have. You're getting far too thin. You're not eating properly, Callum. I blame all that diet muck." Mammy South was shaking her head disapprovingly. Her eyes slid to Gemma, flickered over her and then darted back to the apple of her eye, who was beaming like a loon. "Don't worry, son. I'm here now. I'll look after you."

Err, either Mammy South was going blind in her old age or this was a deliberate dig at Gemma for not looking after her precious firstborn. No way was Cal looking thin! He might not have put on as much weight as Gemma had lately but he was still on the cuddly side. Thin? Diet muck? How dare she? Gemma waited for Cal to grow a set and tell his mother that he was fine, but she would have been waiting a very long time: he seemed perfectly content just to stand there and have his hair ruffled while his mother inspected him for Gemma-inflicted damage.

Thank God she didn't know about the handcuffs!

"Hello Moira," Gemma said eventually, when it became clear that Mammy South wasn't going to bother greeting her. She stitched a smile onto her face, although it probably looked far more like a snarl. "How wonderful to see you."

Moira South grudgingly ripped her attention away from Cal. Her eyes swept Gemma like one of her horse-trading forebears assessing a nag and instantly finding all its faults. Not Irish, not Catholic, not married, not Aoife…

"Hello, Gemma. Grand to see you again. You're looking… well," she said, pointedly.

Gemma gritted her teeth because everybody knew that *well* meant fat. Don't rise to it, she told herself; don't give her the satisfaction.

"You too," she said, so sweetly it was like somebody had dropped a sack of icing sugar in the room. "Welcome back to Kenniston."

"Oi! Mammy!" came a shout from outside. "I need a slash! I'm dying, so I am. Shall I go in the flower pot?"

"Fergus!" shrieked one of the identikit twins, all orphan-Annie red curls and freckles. "You're a disgusting dirty fecker!"

Cal laughed. "Ah, it's grand to see the young ones, Mammy. They're full of fun as always."

Fun wasn't the adjective that Gemma would have used. Mindful of the proving dough and the focaccia, she said, "Cal, why don't you go and show your folks up to their rooms? Then Fergus can use the loo and you can all settle in."

Mammy South's eyes snapped to Gemma.

"Rooms? What is this now, some fancy hotel?" She rounded on Cal. "You're putting your family in a hotel? You're getting rid of us? Are you ashamed?"

"No, Mammy," Cal soothed. "Angel and Laurence have kindly said that you can stay at the big house. There's far more room there and it's much more comfortable. I'll get your things carried up. Dwayne, give us a hand, mate?"

Dwayne, who'd been watching the scene unfold with the kind of attention a cobra gives its prey, nodded and stepped forward – but Mammy South held up her hand and stopped him in his tracks with one hard stare.

"I haven't travelled all this way to be palmed off on your friends," she told Cal. "It's far from stately homes and airs and graces that you were raised, Callum South. No, we are not staying in the big house."

"So where are you going to stay?" Cal asked.

Mammy South raised her doughy chin. "We're family, and isn't Christmas a time for family? Real family, that is." She paused and then looked straight at Gemma. It was the female equivalent of throwing down a glove. "Sure, and where else would we go at Christmas, son? We're going to stay with you!"

Chapter 14

As if things between Gemma and Cal weren't already strained enough, the arrival of Mammy South highlighted everything that had already been driving Gemma wild. It was bad enough seeing the man she loved regressing to a twelve-year-old mummy's boy; no wonder Cal made so much mess and had a total inability to pick his underpants and socks up off the floor, when his mother ran around after him as though he was the Pope, Baby Jesus and Brad bloody Pitt all rolled into one curly-haired package. But it was worse again still being saddled with Mammy South at the Lion Lodge, where she sniffed at the dust, was horrified at the lack of food in the fridge and generally occupied herself by finding fault with everything from the get-go.

It was one thing for Gemma to complain about the damp and the cold and the lukewarm water, given that she lived here and had to put up with it. Yet it was quite another entirely to have Cal's mother snooping through the cupboards and looking as though she had a bad smell under her nose (although she may well have done; the damp in the spare room was pretty shocking), and criticising everything from the way Gemma made tea (so weak – was that an English thing?) to her choice of fairy lights (colours were rather vulgar, but then in England she supposed people did things differently). Gemma wasn't sure what the word was for murdering your almost mother-in-law, but she was pretty sure she'd soon find out.

Thank goodness they only had one guest room and were spared the total carnage of an invasion by the pack of wild creatures otherwise known as Cal's siblings. They'd all ended up staying at Kenniston, much to Dwayne's delight – and Laurence's horror, which was fair enough seeing as the house had only just been restored. Gemma felt his pain, albeit she was certain it was less than hers, as she was being constantly bombarded by Mammy South's disparaging comments. Still, if Laurence insisted on playing the reality-TV game then he really oughtn't to be surprised when it turned around and bit him on the bum. If anyone had taken the time to ask Gemma whether or not it was a good idea to take the entire South clan out of Cork for Christmas, then she would have told them exactly why it was the worst idea since the captain of the *Titanic* said "full steam ahead". If nobody had thought to ask her, then maybe, just maybe, they deserved all they got.

By now Angel would be tearing her long blonde extensions out as the junior members of the South family ran riot through Kenniston. Well, that served her right for going along with the crazy plan of inviting them all for the festive period, and for taking Cal's side over the Christmas and birthday holiday. With any luck, reflected Gemma darkly, Dougal was drinking his way through what was left of the priceless wine cellar, the twins were playing dress-up with Angel's designer wardrobe and the sulky teenage sisters had sneaked off clubbing with Craig and co. while the other brothers went joyriding on the Segway.

Oh dear, Gemma thought despairingly, she was turning into a really nasty person. This was the effect that living her life under the microscope of *Bread and Butlers* was having on her – and why she and Cal had to leave if there was any hope of a future together.

It was now Tuesday afternoon, and although Cal's mother had only been in situ for less than twenty-four hours, already she had *accidentally* rummaged through Gemma and Cal's wardrobe and unearthed the Pulse bag, which had upset her so much that Cal had had to pour her a drink. Apparently she had never seen such filth in her life – and she'd required a serious amount of Baileys to get over the shock of her precious boy living in sin with such a trollop. Mysteriously though, Gemma's copy of *Fifty Shades* had vanished from her bedside table.

Once Mammy South was sufficiently recovered from this trauma, she'd insisted on being driven to the village shop, where she'd purchased all kinds of carbohydrate-laden rubbish that Gemma knew would make Cal put on a stone as soon as he looked at it. Then she'd spent ages clattering around in the kitchen making a concoction out of corned beef and Guinness, which was apparently Cal's favourite, and some sort of suety pudding spotted with currants.

"Sure, but she means well," was all Cal could say when Gemma hissed at him that his mother was totally taking over. Already Gemma had fished a packet of Earl Grey out of the bin, as well as the box of Bran Flakes that she'd been trying to wean Cal onto.

Gemma gave up and left him to eat sausage coddle and soda bread and goodness knows what other stodge his mother had made. She stomped up the drive to Kenniston in a very bad mood indeed, and even the beautiful wintery landscape couldn't cheer her up. There were five days to go until Christmas (counting today), but Gemma didn't think she'd ever felt less festive in her life.

At least the bakery provided some respite. Cal had taken the whole day off to be with his mother (yet another sore point, because Gemma was always pleading with him to have a day off so they could spend some time together), and Daisy and a couple of the other staff were busy filling in for him. The bakery thrummed with industry and Gemma was able to lose herself for a few blissful hours working on her final orders. By the time the sky outside the windows had turned indigo and a big moon was floating over the parkland like a silver balloon, she was feeling slightly better. The last cakes were ready for Dee and that was it; she was finished until the New Year.

"Gemma, darling, there you are!" Lady Daphne strode into the bakery towing a mutinous South twin in each hand, her long aristocratic fingers clamped around their wrists like manacles. "No, Shannon. No, Kathleen! You are staying right with me! I caught them doodling on the walls in the drawing room," she explained with a weary lift of her brows. "What do they think we are? Longleat?"

"There's already pictures on the ceiling, so," muttered Shannon – or was it Kathleen? It was pretty hard to tell: they were identical with their freckles, snub noses and wicked dimpled grins.

Lady Daphne sighed. "That's a trompe l'oeil by Louis Laguerre. He didn't ever paint Sponge Bob, as far as I'm aware. Still, girls, if you're very good there is a blank wall in my bedroom and I love Sponge Bob and Bart Simpson too. You could always paint there if you promise not to touch the other walls?"

The twins cheered. They adored Daphne.

"You make it look so easy," Gemma said enviously.

"Darling, it isn't hard. Just have fun with them," Laurence's mother said. "That's what it's all about, after all, isn't it?"

Was it? Gemma was no longer so sure. Somewhere along the way she'd lost sight of that. There had been a time when she and Cal had laughed non-stop; sometimes they'd each begged the other to relent because their ribs hurt too much and their jaws ached. Now, though, as she stood in the amazing state-of-the-art bakery that they'd designed and built together, with her beautiful cakes all ready to go and battalions of bread baskets lined up waiting for Cal's next batch for a smart New

Forest boutique hotel, she realised she couldn't remember the last time they'd laughed together.

When had it stopped being fun? When had work become more important to Cal than spending time with her?

"We're about to decorate the tree," Daphne was saying. "You're the only one who's missing, so I had to come and find you. Everybody has to join in. It's the tradition."

The Kenniston tree was a big deal. Cut from the estate, it was over ten feet tall and took pride of place in the Great Hall. For the past two Christmases Gemma had loved seeing the tree come to life as everybody from Viscount Laurence to Doris the cleaner looped it with strands of lights and dangled decorations from the spiky limbs. A log fire crackled in the enormous hearth, plates piled high with Gemma's melt-in-the-mouth mince pies emptied in seconds, and the mulled wine flowed. Carols played, people laughed and chatted, and the magic of Christmas filled the room. Decorating the Kenniston tree really meant that the festive season had arrived. Previously Gemma had loved this unofficial Christmas party; she and Cal had handed out the mince pies, scoffed a fair few too, and stolen kisses powdered with sugary pastry crumbs when they'd bumped into each other on their rounds. Once the food had gone they'd road-tested the swathes of mistletoe that had dangled from the chandelier, sipped gloopy mulled wine and then joined in with singing Christmas carols under the tree. Today though, these memories made Gemma's throat clot with sadness. She'd been missing from the gathering and only Lady Daphne had thought to come and find her. Cal hadn't even noticed she wasn't there.

"I know you don't want to be filmed, darling," Lady D continued, "and I promise that you won't be, but you're such a part of our family here. We can't possibly do this without you."

"Decorating the tree! Yay! Come on, Gemma!" cried Shannon and Kathleen – and almost before Gemma knew what was happening they broke free from Daphne and grabbed her hands, tugging her out of the bakery and into the courtyard.

The cold air stung her cheeks and her breath rose like smoke. Stars dusted the sky like glitter and already Jack Frost was scraping the countryside with chilly fingers. Chatter and the strains of carols drifted over from the big house, and as the twins towed her up the steps to the huge entrance hall with its marble floors and sweeping staircase, the Christmas tree was already shimmering with hundreds of white lights. In spite of everything that had happened recently, Gemma's heart lifted. After all, it was Christmas, wasn't it? And everything was always perfect at Christmas. That was part of the magic.

The Great Hall was full of people. The crew were filming like crazy and Gemma didn't blame them one bit because this scene could have come straight from a Richard Curtis movie. Every generic convention was neatly ticked off, from the beautiful Lady Kenniston – Angel Elliott – who looked stunning in a peacock-hued ballgown, to the plethora of quirky characters milling around with arms full of tinsel. All that was missing was Hugh Grant and some very convenient seasonal snowfall.

Big wicker baskets overflowing with baubles and decorations were lined up by the foot of the tree. Gemma was just about to go and help herself to a handful when she caught sight of Cal by the foot of the stairs and her heart turned a somersault. With his golden curls burnished in the soft light and dressed in the moss-green jumper she'd bought him during their first winter together, he was so familiar and dear and totally and utterly Cal that her every cell wanted her to hurl herself into his arms, bury her face in his neck and tell him that nothing else mattered apart from being with him.

It was Christmas, a time for being with the people you loved, and she loved Cal. What else could possibly matter more?

Scooping some decorations from the baskets, Gemma wove her way through the Great Hall towards Cal, willing him to look up and give her that sexy sleepy-eyed smile that always melted her heart, but Cal was engrossed in a discussion with his family. He seemed to be holding Dougal's phone out of reach and staring at it intently while Mammy South harangued him, her mouth opening and shutting like a koi carp's. Several other South siblings were also clustered around, including the twins, who were shrieking that they needed to see.

For some reason a fingernail of unease scratched its way along Gemma's spine. Something was up – not because the Souths were squabbling (squabbling was like breathing to that family), but because Cal's mouth was all twisted and funny looking and he was actually shouting back at Dougal now. Her pulse skittered. Cal never shouted. Usually he was the typical cliché of being so laid back he was horizontal. Something must really be wrong. As she drew nearer to him the Souths' conversation rose above the cheerful strains of "Rocking Around the Christmas Tree". A boom mike hovered nearby like some malevolent bird of prey. It was flanked by two members of the crew armed with Steadicams – but the Souths were far too busy to realise. Gemma was actually starting to wonder whether Cal even noticed the cameras anymore.

"Where the feck did you get it?" Cal was shouting, the iPhone held just out of Dougal's reach.

"Give it back, you fecker!" Dougal shouted back. His face was puce with rage. "That's mine, so! And anyway, it's all over the Internet! It's not my fault. Our Bernie showed me."

Cal whipped round and pinned his gangly sixteen-year-old sister with a furious stare. "And is that so?"

Bernadette South shrugged and put her hands into the universal sign for "whatever", loved by teenagers across the globe.

"Is it?" hollered Cal. Gemma didn't think she'd ever seen him so upset, not even when the Dangers had lost the FA Cup to Chelsea.

"Don't go picking on your sister," boomed Mammy South. "Sure, she's a silly eejit, but Bernie's not the one peddling *filth* on the Interweb. If you want to be angry with anyone, Callum, then it's *her*!"

She spun on her heel and jabbed her finger at Gemma, who'd stopped dead in her tracks. Cal ought to be angry with her? Why? What had she done?

"Is everything all right?" Laurence was asking. Beautifully dressed in a DJ and with his long hair caught back at the nape of his neck, he looked as though he'd stepped out of one of the paintings of Elliott ancestors that lined the walls and rose in measured intervals up the stairs.

"If this is about the, err," Laurence flushed and his pewter-grey gaze couldn't quite meet anyone else's eyes, "the unfortunate handcuffs incident in this week's episode, then I assure you that we had Callum's permission to use it."

What? Gemma's attention snapped to Cal. "You let them use that?" A hot wave of humiliation broke over her. Even her palms prickled with shame. The whole of Britain would know that she'd had to resort to tacky red fluffy handcuffs and glittery body paint to get her boyfriend to look twice at her. "Cal how could you? That was private."

"Nothing's private under the contract Cal's signed for *Bread and Butlers*," piped up Dwayne.

"So I see," said Gemma bleakly. She couldn't believe how hurt she felt. "Thanks a lot, Cal. It's nice to know where your loyalties lie."

"Gem, I'm sorry," said Cal. He stepped forward to reach for her but Gemma held up her hands.

"No, don't try and make out it's all fine, Cal, when it bloody well isn't! 'The contract, the contract' – you're like a broken record. I'm sick of always hearing that excuse! If it hadn't been for you and your bloody contract we wouldn't be in this mess."

"Aw, Gemma, not again," said Cal. He looked close to desperation. "You know I've committed to it. I can't break a contract."

"Don't you dare blame my boy for anything when you're no better than you should be!" Mammy South reared up like a striking cobra and, snatching the iPhone from Cal's grasp, thrust it triumphantly under Gemma's nose. "Now what do you have to say for yourself, my girl?"

Gemma stared at the screen in horrified disbelief. There was a weird rushing in her ears – which was possibly the flapping of chickens' wings as they came home to roost, for here on the iPhone, in full and glorious high-definition technicolour, was a picture of her, wide-eyed and clutching a bright red vibrator in a very suggestive way.

Oh. My. God.

"Oh bollocks!" breathed Angel, who'd shimmied down the ladder and was peering over Gemma's shoulder. To Cal she said, "Some girls snapped us when we were in Truro. You know what it's like."

Cal nodded and smiled hopefully at Gemma, his special sleepy-eyed Cal smile that was just for her – or, more accurately nowadays, her and several million viewers.

"Sure, I'm not complaining about your visit to that shop, Gem. I was just a little put out, so, when I caught Dougal with the picture."

"Can we get rid of it?" Gemma asked Dougal. God, she looked awful. There were at least three chins, and why hadn't anyone told her that in her favourite pink Puffa coat she resembled Miss Piggy? That was going straight to Oxfam.

"No way. The pictures have gone viral," said Dougal, grabbing his phone back from Gemma and scrolling through it with great excitement, "There's a hashtag on Twitter now and chat forums and everything, so! It's way cool."

Gemma did not think that a picture of her holding a dildo was cool in any sense of the word – and neither, judging from the acid-drop-sucking expression on her face, did Cal's mother. Their family priest would have a fit. It would be Hail Marys until the second coming.

"It's all fantastic publicity," Dwayne pointed out helpfully.

Angel nodded excitedly. "This will really boost interest in the live show. Maybe Gemma could even get a lingerie deal with the store? That would be great marketing."

"Jaysus, I don't want my girlfriend blazoned all over the country in her knickers!" Cal exclaimed. "Feck! No way."

"But it's fine on *Bread and Butlers*?" Gemma shot back. "And I'm here, by the way! Don't talk about me like I don't exist!"

"The show's totally different and you know it," snapped Cal. "Jaysus, Gemma, just relax so, will you? It isn't such a big deal anyway."

Gemma shook her head. Had everyone gone completely bonkers here? Or was it just her who cared because, as always, she'd ended up looking like a total idiot?

"It's a big deal to me," she said.

Mammy South gave a martyred sigh. "Sure, Cal, and if you'd only taken your chance with Aoife when you had it. Aoife wouldn't parade around with such filth and shame her family. She's a good girl. When her mammy told me you'd had lunch with her the other day in London I must admit we both got our hopes up."

"Mammy! Jaysus! Will you give it a rest about Aoife?" Cal responded so furiously that his mother paled with surprise. Gemma was amazed too. In all the time they'd been together she'd never once heard Cal stand up to his mother.

"You had lunch with Aoife?" she asked, shocked beyond belief.

"Gemma, she's talking bollocks," Cal said frantically. "It's the South gobshite gene!"

Gemma was no fan of Mammy South but in this case she owed her. The gobshite gene was at least telling the truth.

"You lied to me," Gemma whispered to Cal. There was a dreadful ache where her heart used to be. "You were seeing Aoife all along."

Cal's face was a dead match for the marble staircase. He'd been well and truly dropped in it, and just one look at him told Gemma that he was as guilty as they came. He really had been secretly meeting the beautiful Aoife in London. Gemma hadn't been unjustly suspicious, or going mad or paranoid or any of the other things that he and even Angel had teasingly accused her of. Instead, her instincts had been spot on.

Cal had been lying to her for weeks. Maybe even months. Now it all made sense.

"Gemma, please," Cal said desperately. "It's not what you think."

As she stood in the hall, with carols playing and mulled-wine spices hanging heavy in the air, Gemma realised she'd reached the end of a very long and very hard road. The phone calls, the secrecy, the cleared history, the mysterious trips to London…

"It's exactly what I think," she said sadly.

She spun around and walked away as fast as she could – but Cal, although no longer Premier League fit, was still fast enough to sprint after her. Gemma had only just set foot through the huge doors and into the chilly night when he grabbed her shoulders and pulled her around to face him. His eyes burned down into hers.

"Gemma, I'm asking you to trust me." Cal spoke with an urgency that was at odds with his usual calm demeanour. His hands on her shoulders were holding her tightly as though he was afraid to let her go. "I swear on my life that I have never cheated on you. Yes, I saw Aoife in London but it was for a reason, a really good reason. Jaysus, Gemma, I love you! Please, please trust me. Just for two weeks more."

He was blurring and shimmering in front of her eyes.

"So tell me why you were meeting her," Gemma whispered. "Go on, Cal, tell me."

"I can't," he said.

Gemma swallowed. "Can't? Or won't?"

"Trust me," Cal said softly. "If you love me, you'll trust me. Don't check my phone, my computer, my email, Gemma. Just trust me, like I trust you."

"*I* haven't been sneaking around with my ex," Gemma said. "And if it's so innocent then why don't you just tell me the truth?"

"I can't; not yet. Just give me until the show ends, Gemma. I'm begging you, so I am. Two weeks and then I promise everything will be fine. Just trust me."

It was the same old refrain, over and over again, but this time Gemma knew she was hearing it for the final time.

"I'm sorry, Cal," she said, and now the tears spilled from her eyes. "That just isn't going to work anymore. How can I trust you when you've lied?"

"Gem," Cal's voice was hoarse, "this is *me* you're talking to, *me*. I love you. You have to trust me. If we haven't got trust, what have we got?"

They stared at one another. Snowflakes had started to fall, as cold and as unforgiving as the hurts that were falling between them.

"Nothing," Gemma said sadly. "We've got nothing."

This was the part where Cal was supposed to fight for her, to say that he was sorry, he'd been an eejit, he was only Christmas shopping with Aoife, and that he loved Gemma and couldn't live without her. When he didn't say anything of the sort – his hands sliding helplessly from her shoulders instead – his failure to fight only confirmed what Gemma already knew.

Cal was as guilty as sin.

Gemma fled, her feet skidding over the steps and scrabbling onto the cobbles. Cal didn't make any attempt to follow her, and when she reached the top of the drive he was still there watching her, a curly-haired shadow against a doorway filled with dancing fairy lights. Tears ran down Gemma's cheeks, as sharp as knives in the cold air.

Christmas or not, and even though she still loved Cal with all her heart, there was no way Gemma could stay at Kenniston Hall. If Cal couldn't tell her the truth about what he'd really been up to, then as far as she was concerned they didn't have a future.

They were finished.

Chapter 15

Gemma stormed back up the drive to the Lion Lodge, blinded by tears and snow, and hardly able to breathe by the time she opened her front door. She'd heard people talk about being heartbroken – it was a standard cliché, after all – but until the moment Cal's mother had revealed he'd been meeting Aoife on the quiet, Gemma had thought it was just a turn of phrase. Now she knew differently; there was a dreadful ache in her chest, and a stabbing pain every time she pictured Cal with Aoife. Her heart literally was cracking into little pieces, each as jagged and as cruel as the barbed mackerel hooks the Cornish fishermen used. It was unbearable to know Cal had betrayed her; the worst pain imaginable that her lovely Cal, the man she adored with every fibre of her being, was seeing somebody else – and not just anyone, either, but the beautiful, sainted Aoife.

So much for just being "good friends", Gemma thought furiously as she stormed up to their bedroom. To think she'd believed that old bollocks! How Cal must have been laughing behind her back. And as for telling her that she ought to trust him, as though *she* was the one in the wrong here! Talk about the pot calling the kettle black. He'd just proved beyond all reasonable doubt that he was the one who couldn't be trusted. Cal could talk about contracts and responsibilities and "wait until the New Year" until he was blue in the face; it wouldn't make any difference. He'd lied to her and he wasn't prepared to explain why. That just proved he was as guilty as sin.

Gemma sank onto the bed. She was so tired; it was a deep, dragging exhaustion right down to her bone marrow. What on earth was she supposed to do now? She couldn't stay here, not when Cal was in love with another woman. She'd have to leave. There was no way she could bear being near Cal knowing that he was lost to her forever. It was bad enough that his beloved contract bound him, and that no-areas-barred cameras would be following his every move and recording this drama for the open-jawed public to enjoy. She could see the headlines in *Closer* and *Reveal* already: "Cal's Secret Love!", or maybe "Premier League Cheat!" But worse than all that, it would crucify her to see him and know that his love for her had died.

No. She had to get away, and she had to get away now. There was plenty of time to sleep once she was miles from Kenniston and Cal.

Gemma's tears were still falling as she tugged her suitcase down from the top of the wardrobe. Maybe they'd never stop and she'd be like those people who started hiccupping and were still at it years later? Right now it certainly felt like a distinct possibility. Oblivious to the fine layer of dust and dead spiders, she flung open the lid of her case and began scooping random armfuls of clothes from her wardrobe and stuffing them in, little caring what she took, before grabbing her toothbrush, phone charger and the laptop.

All the time she was doing this her mobile phone rang endlessly. Gemma ignored it until she was finished and she'd lugged the suitcase onto the landing. She knew seeing Cal's picture flashing up would only make her howl even more: it was a shot of him she'd taken on that perfect afternoon at Penmerryn Creek. In this shot Cal was forever frozen in time, a dragonfly in amber of a man balancing on the rotted pontoon and laughing down at her, deep creases fanning out from his twinkling eyes and the sky a perfect cloudless blue above his curly head. The happiness of that afternoon and the love he'd felt for her shone from the shot, worlds away from the harsh words and recriminations of earlier this evening.

Gemma returned to the bedroom and sat on their bed with her head in her hands. She needed to get a hold of herself. That warm sunny afternoon might as well have happened in another lifetime. The Cal who'd made love to her so tenderly, kissing every single freckle on her pale shoulders, wouldn't have dreamed of sneaking off for sleazy weekends in London with his ex-girlfriend. That Cal had loved her, she knew he had, and she'd loved him too. How had things managed to go so wrong?

The slamming of the front door made her jump. *Cal!* cried that foolish, pathetic part of Gemma that was longing for nothing more than him to come striding into the house, sweep her into his arms and tell her that it was huge misunderstanding.

What was she thinking? How on earth could any of this be a misunderstanding? Gemma laughed bitterly at her own stupidity. Of course it wasn't a *misunderstanding*. Mammy South had been perfectly clear that Cal was seeing Aoife – and she'd been thrilled about it too, the evil old boot. Cal hadn't exactly denied it either. *Trust me?* Yeah, right.

Still, if this was Cal and he had an exceptionally good reason, she'd probably forgive him – although he'd have to really grovel first...

"Gemma! Are you upstairs?"

Oh. Angel. Another person who was seriously in Gemma's bad books right now.

Thump. Thump. Thump. For such a slim fairylike creature Angel certainly stomped up the stairs like an elephant. When she appeared in the doorway the reason for this became clear: Angel was wearing a huge pair of Dubarry boots under her ball dress. With her long blonde hair tumbling down from her updo and her cheeks slapped pink by the cold, she looked like she was off to do a photo shoot for Mulberry. Cara Delevingne would probably rock up in a minute too.

"Blimey, your house is cold," said Angel, rubbing her bare upper arms. "No wonder you and Cal never have sex. He'd freeze his bits off."

When it came to the day God handed out diplomacy, Angel had been right at the back of the queue, or sleeping in.

"The reason Cal and I aren't having sex, as you so tactfully just reminded me, is because he's seeing Aoife," Gemma told her. Saying it out loud made her stomach clench and a wave of nausea swept over her, because now this was real.

"Oh, Gemma, what a load of old bollocks," Angel declared. She clomped into the room and hurled herself onto the bed. "Of course he isn't. This is Cal we're talking about. He's not got a cheating bone in his body."

"Of course he hasn't. He's just been secretly meeting his sexy lawyer ex behind my back for a coffee," Gemma said sarcastically. "Silly me."

"I know it doesn't look good," Angel was saying, putting herself right up there to win Understatement of the Year, "but I really think you ought to give the guy the benefit of the doubt. I know there's bound to be a totally innocent explanation."

"Angel, if there was, Cal would have told me." Gemma was certain of this. Why else would Cal hold back? It didn't make sense.

"Maybe he can't tell you?"

"Of course he can't: he's having an affair!" Tired of this circular conversation, Gemma hauled herself onto her feet. "I don't know why you're so keen to stick up for him. You're supposed to be on my side. If Laurence was cheating on you I'd want to throttle him."

"If Loz dared to cheat on me he'd soon be wearing his willy as a new kind of dicky bow," Angel said firmly, with a toss of her blonde mane. The look on her face said that she wasn't kidding either. "Anyway, I'm not taking sides. I just think you should give Cal a chance to explain. Wait until the contract is over for the show."

Arrah! If Gemma heard that phrase again she was going to explode. First Cal and now Angel.

"While the contract's still binding anything Cal says and does is up for grabs," Angel continued. "He's got zero privacy, which means that your relationship with him is totally in the public eye. He knows how much you hate that, babes. Maybe he's waiting until he can speak?"

It was a nice idea but with one fatal flaw.

"The cameras don't follow us home," Gemma reminded her friend. "That was why we moved here."

"It certainly wasn't for the heating," Angel said. Her slender arms were covered in goosebumps and her nose was starting to turn blue. "Can't we go back to the Hall and warm up? I'm starting to feel like Jack in *Titanic*."

Gemma ignored her moaning and, abandoning the bedroom for the landing, began to thump her suitcase down the stairs. "Cal and I can talk in private any time we like when we're at home. If he wanted to talk he'd be here now – but no, he's far too busy filming."

"Filming is his job! It's what he gets paid stupidly big amounts of money to do! Here, let me help with that, for heaven's sake, before you hurt yourself." Angel grabbed the end of the suitcase and together the girls manhandled it down the rest of the narrow stairs. Once they were in the hallway, Angel added, "And FYI, when I left he was having the most almighty row with his harridan of a mother. You should have seen him, Gem! He's furious with her."

Gemma laughed bitterly. "Of course he is. She really dropped him in it." She dragged her case to the door. "He nearly got away with it."

"Not because of that! Because she's been such a bitch to you!" Angel grabbed Gemma's arm and swung her friend round to face her. "You should have heard him; he was wonderful. He told her that he loves you and that if she carries on being so unpleasant and disrespectful she can get straight back on the plane. You're making a big mistake if you walk out on him! Cal loves you. I know he does."

For once Gemma's best friend was serious. The pouty, hair-twirling, designer-crazed Angel was gone and in her place was the razor-sharp and determined woman who ran a successful TV company and who'd managed to convince one of the richest and toughest Russian oligarchs on the planet to help her. For a moment her vehemence made Gemma hesitate. Was Angel right? Ought she to give Cal a chance to explain?

Then again, how many chances did he need? He'd lied about meeting Aoife. What else had he lied about? Where was all the cash from the show going? If Cal's share was "stupidly big", as Angel had said (and with the high ratings the show had enjoyed this year, Gemma had no reason to think this wasn't true), then why was there never any money? What or who was he working so hard for? Why wouldn't Cal level with her about this? And then there were the mysterious phone calls and the wiped browsing history. Gemma's head was spinning from thinking about it all.

It wasn't just this business with Aoife. There was something much deeper going on and Gemma was tired, just so bone tired, of it all. She needed a break to clear her head.

"I need some space," she said wearily. "I can't go on like this. It's impossible."

"You're really leaving him?" Angel asked. Her blue eyes were wide with horror. "Gem, you can't! You mustn't! You love Cal and he loves you! This is mad!"

"If Cal loves me so much, why isn't he here?" Gemma said quietly. There was still a treacherous little part of her that was longing for Cal to stride through the door and put everything right, although with every second that passed this was looking less and less likely.

"Because I said I'd come and talk to you!" Angel cried. "Gem, he doesn't think you're leaving. He was sorting out his mum and then finishing the final shots. He asked me to make sure you were all right."

Typical, Gemma thought. She was second as usual and Cal had farmed out checking on his betrayed and heartbroken girlfriend to somebody else. Enough really was enough.

"I need to get away," she repeated. "I'm not asking anyone's permission, Angel. I'm doing this for my own sanity. If Cal wants to put things right he can tell me the truth. Until that happens I really don't think I want to see him."

"Where are you going?" Angel asked. Her voice trembled.

"Cornwall," Gemma told her. Until that moment she hadn't given any thought to where she was going, but now a plan was taking shape. "I've got that cottage in Rock booked, remember? The one I was hoping to go to with Cal? I may as well make the most of it."

Angel glanced outside. While they'd been talking the snow had started settling, a talcum-powder dusting on the hard earth. The B road beyond the estate was bound to be icy already.

"I'm not going to change your mind, am I?" she said sadly, and Gemma shook her head.

"Only Cal telling the truth could do that."

"And you really can't trust him and wait?" As Angel said this it seemed to Gemma that her best friend couldn't quite look her in the eye. Was she hiding something? Gemma wondered, before giving herself a sharp mental kick. All this business with Aoife was making her paranoid and suspicious – two very unattractive qualities and not ones that she wanted to become a permanent part of her psyche. This was why she had to get away.

"Trust works both ways," Gemma told her. "Cal knows where I'll be if he wants to talk."

Angel nodded. "I'll tell him, Gem, but please…" She paused, looking as though she was about to add something further, before shrugging. "Just give him a chance to explain. I really don't think Cal is the type to cheat."

"They're all the type to cheat," Gemma said despondently. She picked up her mobile. "Don't look so excited – I'm not calling Call: I'm calling a cab to take me to the station. I'll catch the last train and get Dee to pick me up from Bodmin."

"Don't be daft. You'll freeze to death. Look, if you're really sure you want to do this you'd better take the Defender. You're still insured to drive it, so you might as well use it. The keys are in it," Angel said quietly. "I'll borrow a coat and walk back."

That might be a better solution, Gemma reflected. Rather than disturbing Dee so late, perhaps for tonight she could find a budget room somewhere en route; then she could check in to the cottage tomorrow. Together Angel and Gemma carried the suitcase out of the Lion Lodge and to the car. The world was silent and still, except for the whirling snowflakes spinning down to earth in a giddy dance, and when Gemma started the engine the throaty diesel roar made both girls jump.

"My sister's in Rock for Christmas," Angel told Gemma. "I'm going to text her and let her know you'll be there. Talk to Andi about this, Gem. She's always got a solution."

Andi Evans was brilliant and brainy but Gemma knew that even she couldn't solve this problem. Cal was the only person who could do that – by telling her the truth.

As she drove away into the darkness, her heart breaking all over again with every mile that took her further from Cal, Gemma had a dreadful suspicion that Cal wasn't going to do this. That meant only one thing: Gemma Pengelley and Callum South were over for good.

Chapter 16

Seagull Cottage was everything that Gemma had hoped for. It was set just above the slipway, the last dwelling in a picturesque crumpled terrace of fishermen's cottages, and gazed out across the ever-changing waters of the Camel Estuary. Thick walls kept the chill winter wind at bay when it whipped the Atlantic into a stampede of galloping white horses, and clever double glazing meant that you could easily curl up in a window seat and watch the view, your toes toasty thanks to a cute pot-bellied wood burner and state-of-the-art heating. The bespoke kitchen was small but beautifully designed, with glowing walnut work surfaces and an electric Aga that looked the part yet was easier to use than her microwave. The giant sleigh bed nestled under the eaves, a perfect place to snuggle up when the storms rolled in. The roll-top bath just called out to be filled to the brim with Floris bubbles, and wallowed in while sipping champagne from one of the elegant flutes generously supplied by the owners.

Yes, Seagull Cottage really was everything that Gemma had dreamed of – apart from one vital detail: she'd never envisaged being here without Cal. The whole point of this peaceful haven had been that they could spend time together and find themselves again. The reality was, Gemma thought sadly as she pulled on her boots and prepared to wander into the town, they'd never been further apart.

Just as Gemma had predicted, the small seaside town had come to life for Christmas. As she strolled along Rock Road she played a little game for her own amusement, which involved counting how many Range Rovers, Porsche Cayennes and BMW X5s she could see. When she reached double figures before she'd even got to the beach, Gemma gave up. The festive season was certainly here now. The cafés were filled with glossy new arrivals, snugly wrapped in Boden and Hermès scarves and wearing pristine Dubarry boots. The shop tills rang as pasties, local cheeses and organic vegetables filled Cath Kidston cloth shopping bags. Although the snow had melted away the further west Gemma had travelled, it was still bitterly cold – the coldest winter in a decade, according to the weather forecasters – and walking along the beach now, Gemma wondered how Cal was managing at the Lion Lodge. Had he figured out how to coax the asthmatic fan heaters into life? Was he cold in bed without her? Did he miss her as much as she missed him?

She checked her phone for what had to be the millionth time in the past hour, but apart from one text when she'd arrived – a simple message saying that he loved her and wanted her to trust him – there had been nothing. Gemma had fired a quick text back saying that she loved him too but wouldn't be lied to, and since then there had been silence.

Gemma felt sick, so sick that she'd hardly been able to eat a thing since she'd arrived in Rock. The misery diet had to be her most effective yet, she thought glumly. The luxury hamper sat forlorn and unloved on the kitchen table in Seagull Cottage, all the goodies that she'd looked forward to sharing with Cal still wrapped up in red ribbons and glossy paper. He'd have loved that goose-liver pâté, spread on crusty lightly toasted bread, and they would have made a mini picnic in front of the wood burner. Or perhaps they'd just have stayed tucked up in bed with the champagne truffles and mugs of hot chocolate. Even through her sadness Gemma couldn't help smiling; far too much of their spare time was spent enjoying food, and a great part of their working life was spent creating it! No wonder they were both always battling the bulge.

She walked to the end of the ferry pontoon and stared across the water to Padstow. It was a grey afternoon, the estuary whipped into choppy little waves by the icy wind, and a few chilly seagulls were bobbing about and looking rather seasick. The sky above was the same pewter grey as Laurence Elliott's eyes, and clotted with swollen clouds. The world was as cold and as bleak as Gemma felt.

She checked her phone again but the messages folder remained empty. Maybe he was pleased to see the back of her? Perhaps Aoife was already on her way to Kenniston for Christmas? Or would Cal drive up to London and visit her in her smart Docklands flat? (Actually, Gemma had no idea where Aoife lived, but this seemed to suit her chic and rather ice-maiden style persona.) Cal and Aoife would be strolling hand in hand alongside the sluggish grey waters of the Thames and stopping for pastries at a trendy pavement café – laughing as icing sugar dusted their lips, and then kissing away the crumbs…

I have to stop thinking like this, Gemma told herself sternly. If things were over between her and Cal, then torturing herself really wouldn't make her feel better. Unfortunately her plan to come to Cornwall in order to put some space between them was backfiring badly. Rock was the place where Gemma and Cal had first met, and every corner she turned brought back memories. Although the town was wintery, the trees bare of leaves and the colour leached from the sky, in Gemma's mind it was brimming with warmth and vibrancy, as though a piece of tracing paper filled with summer's designs of blue skies and hedgerows freckled with daisies had overlaid the December scene. Her walk took her past the bakery where she'd first met Cal and down to the estuary where he'd almost drowned, before leading her out of the town and past Valhalla, the house he'd rented for that golden summer.

Gemma so wished she could turn back time, if only for a few minutes, and be that girl again – so full of hope (and pasties), and with her lips tender from stolen kisses. Wherever she looked she thought she saw shadows of the people they used to be, and she wanted to run up and tell them to enjoy every second of their Cornish escape before the pressures of television and fame and ex-girlfriends caught up with them.

Trailing through the streets of Rock like a sad ghost of the girl she'd once been was not how Gemma had imagined spending Christmas or the days leading up to her thirtieth birthday. She didn't think she'd ever felt so miserable in her life. How on earth had this happened?

Gemma was due to have supper with her friend Dee later on but she couldn't face being all alone in Seagull Cottage, developing RSI from checking her phone and torturing herself by imagining the wonderful romantic time she could have spent there with Cal. Instead she managed to while away the afternoon by taking the passenger ferry across the Camel to Padstow, where she mooched around the shops before having a coffee and visiting the lobster hatchery. Good. That was a few more Cal-less hours killed, Gemma thought as she queued for the return ferry. The thought of how many more there would be to come was quite simply terrifying. She missed him so much.

By the time she arrived back in Rock it was getting dark. Christmas-tree lights twinkled in the windows of cottages, jewels of colour spilling into the inky water and trembling as the tide shifted restlessly in the estuary. Cold and tired to the marrow, and still with not a word from Cal, Gemma glanced at her watch and saw to her relief that it was time for her to walk up to Dee's for supper. Then she would partake in the televisual equivalent of picking a scab – watching the latest episode of *Bread and Butlers*. Gemma knew that Dee, an ex life coach, thought this a very bad idea, but she was helpless to resist. She had to see Cal, even if it was just on the telly. It was a sad day indeed when the only way she could find out what the man she loved was up to was by watching the very show that had helped to drive them apart.

At least the sea air had worked its magic: by the time she arrived at Dee's house, at the top end of the town and quite a climb from the seafront, Gemma discovered that she was ravenous. She paused at the gate to catch her breath and admire the view. From here the town below looked like a model village and Padstow was just a collection of shimmering lights across the water.

"Don't stand there; you'll die of cold!" Dee called through the open top half of the stable door, where she'd been smoking. She flicked the butt into the garden and sparks fantailed into the darkness.

"Still not quit then?" teased Gemma, and Dee grimaced. An older woman who'd done all sorts, from working as a stockbroker to life coaching to opening a successful bakery, Dee had certainly lived several lives in one. Being organised and thorough in all areas of her life, it drove Dee wild that the one thing she still couldn't get to grips with was her nicotine addiction.

"A girl's got to have some vices," she said.

"Is that your professional opinion or just an excuse?"

"You know me far too well," sighed Dee. "Sod it; I know I have issues with my rather addictive personality. If you can bear to be around an evil smoker, come on in. I've made some mulled wine, and yes alcohol is another vice of mine!"

Vice or not, it was one Gemma was happy to share. Once she was inside Dee's cosy cottage, curled up in a squashy armchair with a glass of wine and a huge plate of pasta, she felt much better. The wood burner had chased away the chill of the night outside, candles threw soft light across the room and carols were playing quietly on the stereo. Gemma started to feel herself relax. That horrible churning sicky feeling, which had plagued her for days, had gone completely – probably because being with Dee, who knew her inside out and was nothing to do with *Bread and Butlers*, was a bit like sinking into a warm bath. It would be OK to cry if she needed to – Dee always had a box of tissues somewhere – and it was a big relief not to have to pretend she was fine. Oddly enough, just knowing this made Gemma feel far less on the brink of hysteria than she had since Mammy South's revelation that Cal had been secretly seeing Aoife.

"So," Dee said finally, once Gemma had mopped up the last of the pasta sauce with a big wad of garlic bread, "do you really think Cal is having an affair with an ex-girlfriend that he last dated when Westlife were still topping the charts and he was yet to start shaving?"

"This is serious, Dee." Gemma swirled her wine and then took a big gulp. It actually tasted far too sweet. Unable to drink any more, she put it aside. "He lied about seeing her in London and even when he's totally caught out he still refuses to give me a good reason. All he could say was 'trust me'."

"So why couldn't you?" Dee asked.

Gemma goggled at her. "Why couldn't I what?"

"Trust him. He's your partner and the man you love, isn't he? So why couldn't you trust him when he told you that nothing was going on?"

"Err, because he lied about seeing her in the first place?" said Gemma. Wasn't it obvious? Some life coach Dee must have been. No wonder she switched to baking. "If he lied about that he must have something to hide."

Dee steepled her fingers. "Maybe; maybe not. Has it occurred to you that it might not be something as cataclysmic as an affair? And that maybe the secret he's keeping isn't his? Maybe it's something to do with this Aoife? Perhaps she has man trouble?"

Actually, no. Gemma hadn't thought of this and she wasn't about to start now. "Cal's my partner; he's supposed to tell me everything," she said firmly. "Besides, Dee, you've not see Aoife O'Shaughnessy. She's not the sort of girl to have problems with guys – they all see her and drool. She looks like an Irish version of Megan Fox."

Her friend raised her eyes to the ceiling in despair. "Do you think your self-esteem still needs a bit of work? I bet you're not doing your mirror affirmations, are you?"

Dee had once given Gemma a load of mantras to chant when she stood in front of the mirror – things like "I love and approve of myself" and "My body is my friend". Gemma had tried, but since most days mirrors were to her what garlic was to vampires, she'd not lasted long.

"Anyway," Gemma carried on sadly, "Cal's mother loves her. She's always wanted him and Aoife to get married. She's best friends with Aoife's mother. It's probably for the best. Mammy South's never liked me."

"Cal loves _you_, Gemma," Dee said. "You're his choice, not his mother's. Anyway, mothers and sons have a complex relationship; just check out some D H Lawrence or ask my boys! I suspect Mammy

South would have an issue with whoever stole her baby away, even this Aoife."

"Hmm." Gemma doubted this very much. "Anyway, it's not just that. Cal's obsessed with work and the show. I booked Seagull Cottage for our Christmas and my thirtieth and he told me to cancel it until the New Year!" She still felt outraged whenever she thought of this. It was just so bloody unreasonable!

Dee said nothing but she did go and pour herself another glass of wine.

"Can you believe that?" Gemma asked when there was no reply. "He wanted to put my birthday on hold until the live Christmas special was in the can. Nice to know where I stand in the general scheme of things. All I ever heard was him saying he was under contract."

"And was he?" asked Dee. She was always one to get straight to the point.

"Well, yes but–"

"So he couldn't just walk away from the show? He'd be breaking a legally binding agreement?"

"Yes, but he could have asked. I'm sure Anton Yuri would have let him take me away for my thirtieth," argued Gemma.

"Which would have meant letting down the rest of the crew?" Dee shook her head. "Gemma, I know you're upset but maybe you ought to try and see things from Cal's perspective? He's being honourable because he's committed to the show. That's a good quality. The other things you've mentioned – the money, the phone calls, this business with Aoife? I can't explain those but I'm sure Cal will. Maybe he's cheating – or maybe you've just added up two and two and made five?

You know him best and you love him, don't you? Surely he deserves the benefit of the doubt?"

Gemma stared at her friend and suddenly she felt as though somebody had pulled out the plug on her nice sink full of righteous anger. Everything was inside out if she looked at it Dee's way. Maybe she had been too hasty? She did love Cal and he'd never let her down before…

"I'm going to call him," she said. "We need to talk."

"Hooray! She's seen sense at long last," said Dee, clapping her hands and grinning. Then she jumped up from her chair as though electrocuted. "Oh my goodness, Gemma! We've been so busy talking we've not noticed the time. If you want to catch your beloved we'd better switch the telly on."

Dee had two teenage boys and consequently a state-of-the-art TV that was the size of a small car and totally at odds with her tiny coastguard's cottage; it made her sitting room look a bit like the bridge of the Starship *Enterprise*. All sorts of strange bits of hardware were rigged up to it, from Xboxes to Wiis to an Apple TV box, which Dee swore did amazing things when she could get it working. There were about eight remote controls for all the myriad equipment. Eventually, once Dee managed to unearth one, she was able to turn the telly on.

It almost took Gemma by surprise to see the people she knew so well and the place where, until recently, she'd lived her life on the small screen for entertainment. The episode was already ten minutes in and they were straight into a scene where Craig and Dougal were hiding on the roof and rolling cigarettes while Mammy South hollered and bellowed down below. Gemma had to admit that the Souths did make good TV. Dwayne was a menace but, give him his due, he knew his stuff. The Christmas-tree decorating incident had already played out, much to her relief. It was painful enough without having it dredged up again.

"No Cal so far," Dee remarked as the adverts played and she brewed coffee so strong it could have won a powerlifting competition. She carried a tray through and, while the latest Marks & Spencer offering was persuading middle England to buy cute swing coats in rich velvet hues and bobble hats with matching scarves, she ripped open a packet of chocolate biscuits and passed the plate to Gemma.

"Maybe he's not on today." Gemma wasn't sure whether she liked this idea or not. She knew Cal had a huge workload to complete. "He might have been in the bakery."

Dee pushed the plunger down and then poured the coffee into two chunky mugs.

"Oh, it's back on," she said, passing Gemma a drink before settling down next to her on the sofa. "Hey! Isn't that Cal?"

Sure enough, the giant screen was filled with Cal's face in glorious and (as Angel was always moaning) totally unforgiving high definition. Gemma's stomach pancake-flipped at the sight of the golden curls, the downturned eyes starred with laughter lines, and that dear freckled face. Was it her imagination or did he look tired? Lucy, their make-up girl, always did a fantastic job, but Gemma thought she could see violet shadows under his eyes and a strained twist to his usually smiling mouth. Her heart knotted with love and it was all she could do not to reach out and touch the screen.

Moments later she was feeling rather differently because as the shot widened it became clear that Cal wasn't on his own. He was in the back of the bakery chatting away merrily to none other than Aoife

O'Shaughnessy. She was perched on the stainless-steel counter, her long racehorse-skinny legs in chunky tights swinging as she tested his latest wares in a way that looked horribly metaphorical. Although the scene was focusing on Daisy's flirting with Craig, Gemma couldn't have given a hoot about them. She couldn't tear her eyes away from Cal and Aoife.

She simply couldn't believe it. Of all the barefaced cheek! Gemma had barely been gone for two minutes and already Cal had moved his ex in. *And* she was sitting on the counter where Gemma was always being told off for perching! *And*, just to add insult to injury, the camera absolutely adored her. Of course it bloody did. Why not? Everyone else was in the Aoife fan club.

How could Angel let the production team invite Aoife onto the show when she knew how upset Gemma was? Some friend she'd turned out to be. Gemma could hardly bear to watch, but it was the same morbid fascination she'd had as a child watching *Doctor Who*; she simply couldn't look away, even though what she was watching was bound to give her nightmares.

Aoife and Cal might only be chatting about family and Ireland, but as far as Gemma was concerned they may as well have been having sex on the bakery's worktops. It couldn't be clearer that Cal was moving on.

Dee turned to Gemma. Her hazel eyes were glittering with anger.

"It's lucky I'm a better baker than I am a life coach," she said furiously. "Honey, I take it all back. That man doesn't deserve the benefit of the doubt at all. What he deserves is a bloody big smack in the gob."

And Gemma, with her chocolate biscuit melting in her shaking hand, couldn't have agreed more.

Chapter 17

"Hiding in your bedroom isn't going to make you feel any better, my girl. You've had a day of moping around. Now you need to get up and get some fresh air!"

Demelza Pengelley ripped open the bedroom curtains and whipped off the duvet with the practised flourish of a woman who'd spent years rousing reluctant teenagers for school and making sure her husband was up at first light to milk the cows. Just for good measure she flung open the bedroom window too, so that frosty air laden with the tang of salt and seaweed from the estuary could give her daughter a good pummelling.

Gemma buried her face in the pillow. She'd been in bed ever since abandoning the torture of *the Christmas that should have been* in Seagull Cottage and fleeing home to the family farm. Quite honestly she didn't see why she shouldn't stay in bed for the next ten years. What was there to get up for? Her heart was in pieces and whenever she thought of Cal and Aoife together she felt sick. The last thing she felt like doing was getting some fresh air. All she wanted to do was turn her face to the wall and be left in peace to slip into a Catherine Earnshaw style decline. That's what the heroines of all those gothic novels were allowed to do, so why not her?

But, unlike Gemma, most heroines of gothic literature didn't have a Cornish farmer's wife as a mother. Demelza Pengelley didn't do moping or declining or feeling sorry for yourself. Instead she was a fully signed up member of the Snap Out of It school of thought. As a child Gemma had never been allowed to lie in bed, and that wasn't about to change just because she was nearly thirty. She supposed she ought to count herself lucky she'd been left alone this long.

"Come on, love," said her mother, a little less briskly. The bed creaked and sank as she sat down next to Gemma and put her hand on her daughter's shoulder. "This isn't doing you any good at all and it certainly won't bring Cal back."

At the mention of his name Gemma bit back a sob. Everything had fallen apart with such speed that she felt dizzy. Was it only a few days ago that they'd been scrapping over the hot-water bottle and having fun with the silly Santa costume? So much had happened since then, and none of it good. How had it all gone so wrong? Why was she in her old single bed in her teenage bedroom, surrounded by faded curling posters of Take That from the first time around and dusty once-treasured knick-knacks, instead of snuggled up in Cal's arms under the eaves of Seagull Cottage?

After seeing Aoife on the show, Gemma had fired off a furious text to Cal, telling him exactly what she thought of him and his cheating ways. Anger-texting was always fatal, second only to drunken eBaying, and she had then waited for his reply, her nails practically chewed to the quick. When nothing came back she wasn't sure whether to be even angrier or relieved. Now though, she was just sad to her bones because it was obvious that Cal didn't even care enough to reply.

"It's a beautiful day outside," Demelza Pengelley was saying gently. Her work-roughened fingers rose to smooth Gemma's hair away from her damp cheeks. "Sweetheart, I know you're upset about Callum but lying in bed isn't going to help; it really isn't. Get up, have a shower and then go for a walk. You'll feel better, I promise."

Would she? Gemma couldn't imagine how, unless she hurled herself Ophelia-style into the creek. Still, without her duvet to burrow under, bed was certainly less appealing, and the birdsong beyond the window was a better soundtrack than her own miserable internal monologue.

"And it's Christmas Eve today," added her mother. "The hunt will be out. You may even catch a glimpse of it if you walk through the woods. It's a drag one these days, of course, but it's still quite some sight."

Hunting was a big part of rural life and Gemma's father and brothers had all whipped in over the years. Gemma didn't ride herself, but lots of her friends did and it might be fun to catch a glimpse of them. There was something very Christmassy about seeing hounds in full flight across the wintery stubbled fields, followed by riders in hunting pink, while the master's horn sounded. Most of the village would already be at the meet, which was always held at the local pub, and by now everyone would be working through the mulled wine and mince pies and feeling very festive. She wondered whether Cal had finished his final batch of mince pies for that big hotel in Lyndhurst...

Oh no. Cal again. Gemma's eyes filled anew. Would she ever be able to go more than a few minutes without thinking of him? It was like her brain had Cal Tourette's and was determined to mention him at every available opportunity, whether she liked it or not. Maybe her mother was right? A stomp through the countryside might help. At least it would be some exercise. Lolling about in bed was all very well in fiction but in reality it couldn't be doing her figure any favours at all. Even after several days on the heartbreak diet, the bottoms of her pyjamas were a little too tight, which seemed very unfair. Life really did have it in for her.

On the other hand, getting up and moving around suddenly felt as though it would require effort of Herculean proportions.

She closed her eyes. "Can't I just stay here?"

"No you can't just stay in bed! You are getting up, my girl, and doing something! You're not just going to stay in bed all day moping about Cal." Now the pillow was tugged away too, leaving Gemma nowhere to hide. Opening her eyes she saw her mother silhouetted against the brightness of the day, her hands on her hips and a determined expression on her face. "Listen to me, Gemma Pengelley! Have I brought you up to lie around sobbing over a man? Or are you made of stronger stuff? Where's your girl power?"

Her mother looked so fierce that Gemma laughed in spite of herself. "I think it's still in the nineties with the Spice Girls, Mum!"

"Time you dragged it into the twenty-first century then," said her mother tartly. "Think about it this way: do you think Cal is lying in bed weeping about you?"

Gemma was trying very hard not to think what Cal might be doing in bed, but she had to admit that lying there sobbing over her was probably not high on his to-do list.

"So don't give him the satisfaction of wasting a second longer on him," continued her mother.

She could have been a little more sympathetic, Gemma thought. In fact, this went for her entire family, none of whom seemed particularly concerned that the love of her life had been cheating on her. Weren't fathers meant to defend their daughters' honour? She'd seen her father more upset when the Cornish Pirates lost a rugby game than he was when he'd learned about Cal.

"Ah well, you can't odds it," he'd said with a shrug, and that had been that. Matter closed.

Her brothers Dave and Kev, about as sensitive and subtle as Miley Cyrus's wrecking ball, weren't much use either. When she'd arrived home in a mess of tears and snot, Kev had just looked awkward and offered to take her to the pub, while Dave had been dim enough to start sticking up for Cal – before Demelza had shut him up with one of her famous looks. From that point on, no matter how hard Gemma had tried to get them to join in with a spot of Cal-bashing, nobody had seemed that bothered. Great. Thanks for the support, family.

"Now, I'm going into Bodmin to grab some last-minute bits from Asda," Demelza was saying. "You can either come and push the trolley with me or you can go for a walk. It's your choice."

"Some choice," Gemma grumbled. The thought of having her shins bumped and bruised by shoppers suffering trolley rage, and her eardrums assaulted by wailing children high as kites on E-numbers and pre-Santa excitement, was not appealing. "I'll go for a walk."

She hauled herself out of bed and dragged herself into the shower, where she attacked her greasy hair with some ancient shampoo and did her best to scrub the misery away with a flannel. By the time she was downstairs and drying her hair by the Aga, Gemma had to grudgingly admit that she did feel more human. There was something about being clean and dressed that made her feel slightly more in control and as though she was returning from the strange twilight world of sobbing. The churning, washing-machine-on-spin-cycle sick feeling was receding too, and she even managed to eat a bacon sandwich. She checked her phone several times but there was still no message from Cal. However, there were three from Angel, asking her to call. Gemma's finger hovered over the read button for a moment before diving to delete the lot. Much as she loved Angel, her friend had let her down too. Gemma knew that Angel would be aware that Aoife had been filmed, and she didn't want to hear what her excuses would be for having Cal's new woman on the show. With Angel it all came down to one thing, didn't it? Pushing the ratings up and making more money for Kenniston. Friends clearly came into a poor second place these days.

Gemma stashed her plate in the dishwasher and, wandering into the boot room, selected the least filthy pair of Hunter wellies, an elderly wax jacket and a pink woolly Animal hat complete with earflaps. It was hardly the country shabby-chic look that Angel pulled off so effortlessly, but then Gemma wasn't about to pose prettily by an Emma Bridgewater tea set for *Marie Claire*; she was going to stomp through a farmyard covered in cow muck, slosh through mud and stride across fields. If she looked like Elmer Fudd in drag then so be it. Besides, it wasn't as though anyone apart from a rabbit or the odd crow would be looking.

Her mother had been right: it was a glorious winter's day, with the low sun bright and the sky cobalt blue. Whistling to the farm dogs, Gemma set out along the bridleway that hugged her father's big maize field for a mile before it climbed a hill and then plunged back below into a spinney. There was a fantastic view of the estuary from the crest of the hill; if you cricked your neck enough you could even see a slice of the sea and the higgledy-piggledy rooftops of Fowey. The sea always lifted Gemma's spirits, and the more she climbed the better she felt. The dogs ran in front of her, zigzagging with great enthusiasm as they explored all the lovely scents, and sometimes streaking into the fields after a surprised rabbit.

Halfway up the hillside, Gemma paused to catch her breath and waited for the dogs to coming tearing back. She was higher now and could see down to where the green waters of the creek met the deeper blues of the estuary by Penmerryn Cottage. A black car was parked by the house and smoke coiled up from the chimney; Scary Bob Woman was in situ then. Gemma pictured the new owners arriving for their first Christmas there, all excited and London glossy, and tried her hardest to superimpose images of them unwrapping presents by a designer tree over her memories of being there with Cal. It didn't work. All she could see was his face above hers, and the broken beams of the roof framing the blue summer sky before he leaned in and kissed her.

This wasn't helping. Gemma turned her back on the creek and continued to climb. Soon her breaths were coming in sharp pants as the path grew steeper and she broke through the trees to the top. There was Fowey, a miniature toy town balanced precariously on the side of a steep valley, and just beyond it a blue slice of sea glittering in the winter sunshine. Maybe she'd drive there later on and have a last-minute look around the shops for Christmas presents? When all else failed, retail therapy was always an option.

At the top of the hill was another big field, fallow now but usually growing wheat that rippled like an inland sea during the summer months. The bridleway skirted it and then began a slow descent back towards the farm. Gemma was just meandering along, lost in her own sad thoughts, when the drumming of hoof beats announced a horse rider heading towards her at speed. She just had time to flatten herself against the hedge when a large grey hunter charged by, loud snorts piercing the stillness and egg-white foam flying from its mouth. The horse, spotting Gemma lurking in the hedge, did the most enormous sideways spook, but its rider scarcely moved in the saddle, collecting the animal with just the slightest closing of strong fingers on the reins.

"Shh, it's OK, mate. I've got you," the rider said gently. He leaned forward and smoothed the horse's neck. "Ssh, Solo, steady boy."

"Sorry; he saw me and I startled him," Gemma apologised, stepping forward and squinting up at the person on horseback. The sun was low in the sky and as she peered up at the rider it was hard to distinguish his features against the brightness. She reached up and patted horse's steaming neck. "That was some pace you were going at."

The man grinned. "Solo and I are both scared of the dark, so we don't hang about. Apparently there are all sorts of people lurking in hedges."

Gemma smiled at his teasing. His voice was warm, a rich West Country burr mixed with a drawl she couldn't quite identify. It certainly made a nice change from an Irish accent, she told herself firmly, and with his long muscular denim-clad legs wrapped around the horse and his strong arms containing over half a tonne of prancing animal, he was certainly easy on the eye. Was this a local guy then?

The horse stepped forward and the shade of the hedge fell across the rider. It was still hard to see who he was under the jockey skull, but his hair was an unexpected white blond and wide green eyes danced in a face that was surprisingly tanned for Cornwall in December. Bloody hell, he was hot, whoever he was. Sod the Victorian gothic novels. This was a Jilly Cooper hero come to life.

"Have you got far to go?" she asked politely, trying to ignore her skittering pulse. She was still broken-hearted, of course, but a girl could look couldn't she?

And anyway, Cal was with Aoife now and bound to be doing far more than looking. Maybe she should bat her eyelids a bit (it always worked for Angel), or toss her hair, although this was easier said than done with a big hat on. It was typical, Gemma thought, that she should meet Mr Gorgeous just when she was bundled up like an Eskimo.

The rider looked down at her and then laughed. Hang on; there was something rather familiar about that sound. She'd heard it before a long time ago…

"Come on, Gemma – you know Mum and Dad's farm is next door to yours. You haven't been up country that long," the rider said. Amusement laced his words and he laughed all the more when Gemma's mouth literally fell open. "It's me: Rob."

Chink, chink. The penny didn't just drop. It plummeted out of the sky and walloped Gemma right on the top of her bobble hat.

"Rob!" she gasped. "I'm so sorry; I didn't recognise you in the hat!"

This wasn't a lie but it wasn't one hundred percent true either, because Gemma wasn't convinced she'd have recognised him without the hat anyway. The last time she'd seen Rob had been when they'd left school and he'd been a dead ringer for the *Where's Wally* character, only a bit skinnier and definitely spottier. They'd travelled to school together on the bus every day, not out of any real choice but because they'd both got on at the same location. For five years Rob had hardly uttered a word to Gemma, and it had been a great relief when the last (silent) wait at the end of the lane had been over. She'd heard general bits of news about him over the years – their mothers were friends and the farming community was a small one – but they'd not bumped into one another. The last she'd heard, Rob had been living in Australia and working on a sheep station. That explained the accent then.

"I'm hurt. I recognised you straight away in yours," Rob teased. At least, Gemma hoped he was teasing. He had to know that he'd metamorphosed into Adonis since they'd stood in awkward silence at the bus stop all those years ago. He ran his hand down the horse's neck and looked at her askance through thick lashes. "But then, I always did notice you more than you noticed me, Gemma Pengelley."

Gemma shook her head because this was blatantly untrue. "Hardly! You ignored me every day for five years. In fact, I'm amazed you're talking to me now."

Looking more carefully at him, Gemma noticed that his shy smile was the same, only now it carved deep dimples in his stubbled cheeks. Somewhere inside Gemma, something yawned and stretched. Oh. That didn't feel like indigestion from bolting down a bacon sandwich. It felt more like desire.

"Solo's getting cold," Rob said. "He's clipped and I need to take him back and rug him up before he chills. Otherwise, I'd love nothing more than to tell you exactly why I never spoke to you for five years." His gaze held Gemma's as he gathered up the reins. "Are you free this evening? I know it's Christmas Eve and you're probably really busy, but if not do you fancy a drink at The Schooner and a chat about the good old silent days?"

Now it was Gemma's turn to be struck dumb. Was this gorgeous man, who in her mind she just couldn't equate to spotty, sullen Rob, seriously asking her to go for a drink with him?

"Only if you want to, of course," Rob added. The horse, impatient for his stable and a bran mash, began to fidget. "I know I wasn't always the best company in the past."

For a moment Gemma dithered, torn between wanting to find out more about her old school-bus buddy and a ridiculous nagging sensation that she was being disloyal to Cal. *WTF?* she told herself sharply. Firstly this was just a drink with a neighbour and secondly Cal was seeing Aoife anyway. She didn't owe him anything.

Not a bean.

"I'd love to, Rob, thanks!" she replied, before she could bottle out and change her mind – not that she would anyway, once she saw the big smile that crinkled his eyes and made those cute dimples dance in his cheeks.

"Great. I'll pick you up at seven," said Rob. "And wear the hat so I can recognise you!"

He winked at her before his heels bobbed against the horse's flanks and both man and beast surged forward like something out of a legend. Gemma watched as Rob cantered away across the field and popped over the five-bar gate that led to his father's land; her heart was thudding in time with the hooves.

Terror or excitement? It was hard to say, but there was one thing of which Gemma was certain: she was very glad she'd listened to her mother and gone for a walk. Maybe this Christmas wasn't going to be such a disaster after all?

Chapter 18

"You look better. There's colour in your cheeks and you're smiling! I knew a walk would do you good."

Demelza Pengelley beamed at her daughter, whose return had been preceded by the eager dogs dashing into the kitchen before Gemma had even managed to step inside the boot room to change her footwear. Demelza was standing by the sink, busy preparing sprouts for the Christmas dinner. An enormous turkey, one of the ten that the Pengelleys raised every year especially for the festive period, was trussed up in a baking tray, and a mound of potatoes awaited peeling.

Gemma was pretty sure that her glowing cheeks and smiling face had more to do with bumping into Rob Tremaine in his new incarnation as sex god than it did with the bracing cold. She'd replayed their conversation all the way back to the farm and now she could hardly wait until seven o'clock.

"You were right. I feel much better for getting some fresh air," she agreed. "It was just what I needed."

Gemma's younger brother Dave was sitting at the big kitchen table and hacking at a side of cold ham, alternating chunks of juicy pink meat between his own plate and the salivating dogs now at his feet, while his girlfriend Kirsty flicked through *Reveal* and then another magazine. Gemma only just stopped herself in time from groaning out loud. Although Kirsty was very sweet and very pretty, she was as thick as two short planks and obsessed with all things celebrity. Gemma wouldn't get a minute's peace until Kirsty knew exactly what perfume Angel wore (Alien) and where she got her hair done (classified).

"Did I see you chatting to Rob Tremaine just now?" Dave asked Gemma. He lobbed a hunk of meat to the dogs, sending them into a frenzy beneath the table.

Luckily for her son, this question distracted Demelza from what he was doing to the Boxing Day ham.

"He was riding that grey hunter," Dave said, before Gemma could even get a word in. "You know the one, Ma, the sixteen-two? Jumps like a stag and used to belong to the Shakerleys near Polpen? He was riding it up the top field when I was checking the cows."

Honestly, thought Gemma, now she really knew she was back in Cornwall. You couldn't sneeze without somebody in the next village knowing about it. Who needed reality television when you lived here?

"Yes, that was him," she said, in what was hopefully a nonchalant manner. All those years of acting were coming in very useful after all. "It was nice to catch up after so long. We're going to go for a drink later at The Schooner if anyone wants to come."

"He's not been back very long," said Demelza, dropping the final sprouts into a bag ready for the fridge. "He's had to come back from Australia because his father's had a stroke and there's no way Mary Tremaine can manage the farm by herself."

"He was running a sheep station the size of Cornwall," added Dave in awe and looking wistful. "They used helicopters to round them up, apparently. I wonder…"

"We don't need one here, not with only fifty ewes," Demelza said firmly, before her son could get carried away. Sprouts done, she turned her attention to the turkey. All trussed up like something from that *Fifty Shades* book, which Gemma had never seen again after Mammy South had accidentally wandered into her and Cal's bedroom, tomorrow it would be stuffed with the secret Pengelley parsley-stuffing mix. Gemma's mouth watered at the thought. Rob had had a great effect on her. She no longer felt at all queasy. In fact she was ravenous.

"Cal called, by the way," her mother said, seeming suddenly fascinated by the turkey's rear end rather than meeting her daughter's eye. "And before you fly off the handle that he's not rung sooner, he says that he'd lost his mobile. He's only just found it again; apparently you haven't been answering yours. He says can you call him?"

"How convenient," said Gemma. How hard would it have been for Cal to borrow Angel's phone? Then she remembered all the calls from her best friend that she'd ignored. Oh. So he had been trying to get in touch after all. She hadn't taken her phone on the walk and, amazingly, she'd not checked it since she'd come home either. Rob had helped to take her mind off that.

"He sent you some flowers too," piped up Kirsty. "We've put them in the sink in the utility room. They're gorgeous. He must still like you. That thing with Fifi is rubbish. I don't believe it."

"Fifi?" Gemma knew that Kirsty was quite low wattage, but getting names wrong was something else. Fifi was Cal's pneumatic page-three ex ("Sure, Gemma, every footballer has one, so; it's a right of passage, like a hot tub and a Ferrari") and they'd been over for ages before he and Gemma had got together. She sometimes appeared on *Bread and Butlers* because it threw the builders into chaos and she was unintentionally very funny. "You mean Aoife."

Kirsty shook her head. "Eh? Who's that? No, Fifi Royale from *Roller-Skating Celebs*. Look! It's in my magazine. They're talking about body language."

If Gemma had learned one thing over the time that she'd been involved with reality TV, then it was to never read the celebrity press. In her experience you were likely to find your dress sense pulled to pieces in a "What Were They Thinking?" spread, see your fat bits on display or discover that your relationship was on the rocks. It was a sure sign of how bad things were, then, that she practically wrestled the magazine from Kirsty to read about how the live episode of *Bread and Butlers* on Christmas Day would be featuring Fifi as Callum South's dinner date. This was her first mistake. There was a picture of Cal and Fifi when they were together back in his Premier League days; in it, Cal was very buff and Fifi looked as though two bald men were having a fight down her very tight dress. Cal's eyes were practically out on stalks.

Love Rekindled? screamed the headline.

Devastated by the departure of his long-term girlfriend, Callum South will be comforted this Christmas by old flame Fifi Royale.

"Fifi Royale my arse," seethed Gemma. "Everyone knows her real name is Jane Clark."

Anyway, never mind Fifi Fluff-Brains. Where was Aoife? None of this made any sense. Bewildered, she read on with the article, which was her second mistake. It was a lot of made-up nonsense about how Cal and Fifi had been torn apart when he went to play for the Dangers while she pursued a Hollywood career, and how she was spending Christmas with him at Kenniston Hall as they rekindled their romance. A so-called body-language expert had analysed the picture and declared that they were "sizzling", and a pretty pseudo-psychologist had assessed their chances of love success – "very high", apparently. Even though she knew it was all rubbish, most of it probably dictated line by line by

Fifi's agent, just reading it made Gemma feel ill. The thought of Cal with anyone who wasn't her was unbearable.

"It's a load of bollocks," she said, slamming the magazine back on the table. "This is exactly why I didn't want us to be involved with the show anymore."

"And if Cal was seeing her, you'd be upset?" Demelza asked. "I mean, you've told us it's over, but that's not the impression I have."

"He was seeing Aoife!" Gemma cried. Her head was spinning with confusion.

"So you say. He denies it," Demelza said, wiping her hands and turning her attention to the potatoes. Kirsty, who was eyeing Gemma rather warily, abandoned the magazine to help.

"Technically you've left him, so technically he's not doing anything wrong even if he is seeing her," Dave pointed out. He hacked off another chunk of ham, chewing it thoughtfully before saying slowly, "Sis, you've left your man alone at Christmas with a glamour model who's got boobs bigger than my head. I'm no expert, but I'd say that isn't your smartest move yet."

With a howl of despair, Gemma fled the kitchen and bolted up to her bedroom. Snatching up her mobile phone she saw that there were five missed calls from Cal and a rash of texts too. Before she could stop herself she was calling him back, a volcano of rage about to erupt.

Cal answered on the first ring. "Gemma, thank God, darlin'! I've been so worried."

"I can tell," Gemma said coolly. "Fifi *and* Aoife, Cal? I don't know how you've had time to miss me."

"Come on, Gems! That's all bollocks, so it is. You know that."

Gemma was prepared to concede that Fifi was nonsense, but Aoife? She hurled herself down on the bed and stared across at Robbie Williams, who was eyeballing her in a very cheeky way. God, thought Gemma, even Robbie was married and settled down these days. What on earth was wrong with Cal?

"So why was Aoife in the bakery?" she demanded. "Devon's a bloody long way for her to go for a loaf of bread."

Cal was silent for a moment. "I can't tell you over the phone," he said finally.

"Why? Are they filming you talking to me? Or is Anton Yuri tapping the phones now? That ex-KGB stuff wasn't a rumour?"

"No, Gem, none of that. It's just not something I can talk about while I'm here. I need to tell you in person. And I will, as soon as the show is in the can, I promise. Can't you just come back here until then? As soon as the New Year arrives it's all going to be different, I swear."

Not this again. "So you keep saying, but in the meantime you won't give me a good reason why your ex, who you claim to never see, was caught on camera, or why you were meeting her secretly. I'm referring to Aoife by the way, Cal, although I guess I could have been talking about Fifi Royale too."

"Aoife or Fifi? Aw, Jaysus, come on Gemma, make your mind up. Which one am I meant to be shagging?" Cal asked wearily. Gemma could picture perfectly how he was tugging at his curls in frustration. "I know it looks bad but I love you, Gemma, and everything I'm doing, everything I've done, I've done because I truly thought it was best for us." He paused and, when she didn't reply, sighed. "Clearly I was wrong."

Gemma was quiet because she was too sad to speak. She loved Cal too, but there was so much that seemed to have got in the way recently that she wasn't sure how they could ever get past it. This certainly wouldn't happen while he was so many miles away and on the end of a phone. They needed to be together so that they could talk – really talk, and properly too, without the distractions of other people or the business. All these snatched half-conversations, with more things left unsaid and silences all too quickly filled by doubts and shadows, were part of the problem. Suddenly Gemma knew what the answer was.

"Come here, Cal," she whispered. "I miss you so much. Please babe, just get in the car and come to the farm. It's Christmas Eve and I want to spend it with you. That's all I want. I don't care about birthdays or presents. I just want us to be us again."

But no sooner had she said this than Gemma knew she was wasting her time. It was the same discussion they'd been having for months.

"I can't," Cal said with another sigh. "You know I can't. I have to appear in the live show tomorrow. It's—"

"In your contract; yes, I know. You keep telling me." Gemma closed her eyes in defeat. "I know you can't break it."

"I don't want to break it!" Cal said. He sounded annoyed now. "Sure, and I'd hoped you knew me a bit better than this, Gemma. When I give my word and make a commitment, I keep to it. It doesn't mean I love you any the less. In fact, it means I love you more."

"So much you can't or won't explain why your ex-girlfriend has mysteriously arrived now I've left?" she shot back.

"Feck, I know it looks bad but I'll explain about Aoife the next time I see you, Gemma. I promise. It won't be long."

Gemma walked to the window and looked out over the countryside. It was twilight now; bats were flitting from the barns and a slice of moon hung over the hillside, throwing silvery beams across the roof of the Tremaines' house on the far side of the valley. Rob's smiling face flashed through her vision. If Cal could spend time with Fifi and Aoife, then why shouldn't she spend time with an old school friend?

"Fine," she said. "We'll talk after Christmas."

"You could come back here?" Cal suggested hopefully. "I know Mammy can be a devil at times and the kids are a bunch of gobshites, but we miss you, we really do. *I* miss you, Gems. We could have Christmas together, just you and I, once the show is over. Celebrate your birthday properly? Sure, I'll even try that handcuff thing again if you like?"

Gemma almost laughed before she remembered that she was cross with him. Cal was very good at talking her around; the Blarney Stone was probably yet another thing he'd snogged behind her back.

"Cal, until you can tell me why you were secretly seeing your ex and lying to me, there is no you and I." Gemma was adamant on this and she wasn't backing down. "If you can tell me right now what's honestly been going on then I'll jump in the car and drive to Kenniston straight away. Can you do that?"

There was silence and Gemma's heart sank like a stone tossed into the creek. That was her answer then.

"I'll tell you when I see you," Cal repeated. He had a stubborn streak, that was for sure, and Gemma had often been a little afraid that he was more like Mammy South than she'd realised. "Just watch the show tomorrow, Gemma. Please? We'll talk afterwards."

He wasn't coming. She'd pleaded with him, told him what she needed to know, but Cal hadn't budged an inch. He'd refused yet again to explain why he was seeing Aoife, and it was clear to Gemma exactly where she stood in Cal's list of priorities. Watch the show? The show that had driven them apart?

She'd rather be locked in a broom cupboard with Mammy South!

"Happy Christmas, Cal," Gemma said softly. "I hope you have a lovely day."

Before Cal could draw breath to reply, she ended the call. When the phone rang back almost instantly Gemma turned it off and shoved it in a drawer. There it would stay, she resolved, with a determination that actually surprised her. She guessed her tears were all cried out now. Besides, Cal had made his choices clear. He could have told her the truth about Aoife – and if there'd been an innocent explanation, Gemma was sure he would have done. Why else would he carry on prolonging this misery if there was any other solution? It made absolutely no sense. He really must have had an affair with Aoife.

Well, to use a seasonal metaphor, what was sauce for the goose was sauce for the gander, Gemma decided. Who said that she had to spend Christmas and her birthday on her own? In a couple of hours she would be in the pub with the newly gorgeous vision that was her old friend Rob, drinking mulled wine, listening to Slade and without an Irish mammy or ex-girlfriend in sight. She didn't need Callum South to have fun, did she?

It was time she had a bath, dug an old party frock out of the wardrobe and got into the Christmas spirit. After all, a girl was only thirty once.

Chapter 19

Although Gemma's heart still twisted every time she thought of Cal, being in The Schooner on Christmas Eve with Rob Tremaine was certainly making her feel much better. With her mobile stowed safely in her bedroom drawer, rendering her totally incommunicado, and all dark thoughts of Cal and Aoife forcefully shaken off, Gemma was determined to enjoy her evening out.

The pub, a crumpled stone building with crazy sloping floors and low dark beams that had been the undoing of many a tall and drunken visitor, was on the bank of the River Fowey and a hotspot for locals and second-homers alike. In the years that Gemma had been away, The Schooner, like much of Cornwall, had undergone a radical transformation. Having previously been a dark and cave-like smoke-filled haunt for fishermen and farmers, who'd usually gathered by the end of the bar playing dice or eating bar snacks, it had undergone a makeover and was now whitewashed, airy and lit softly with LED spots and white fairy lights. The sausage and chips in a basket, which had been Gemma's personal favourite, were long gone; instead, chalk boards in swirling cursive script boasted the kind of gourmet menus more often seen in Kensington. Even the cider, which had once been a local scrumpy so potent it could double as an anaesthetic should the need arise, had been exchanged for pear or cherry imposters in funky corked bottles.

"I kind of miss the sticky floor and the fag ends," Rob said wistfully as he guided Gemma through the laughing groups of second-homers who were hogging all the tables by the window. His hand rested on the small of her back and he was taking great care that nobody pushed or shoved her. The awkward boy had certainly grown into a real gentleman, Gemma decided – and one who was sweetly oblivious to how many women threw admiring glances in his direction. Not that she blamed them. Although Rob was dressed casually in charcoal cords and a sea-green shirt that echoed the colour of his eyes, his tall, strong body and air of being totally comfortable in his own skin gave him a powerful presence. Gemma was used to people staring when she was out and about with Cal, but this was something else again.

"Please tell me they kept the Pac-Man table?" she said hopefully. As teenagers it had been a rite of passage to drink scrumpy and play Pac-Man. Gemma couldn't count how many nights she and her friends had spent bent over the machine, steering a yellow blob towards cherries while eking out one drink and praying that their parents didn't come in and freak.

Rob smiled at her indulgently. "You've been away even longer than me, haven't you? I think that was claimed by a museum years ago. Sorry, Gemma, I'm afraid you're going to have to talk to me – but I promise my conversational skills have improved since the school bus."

It was on the tip of Gemma's tongue to point out that Rob's conversational skills weren't the only things that had improved, but luckily she stopped herself just in time. Once Rob had bought them both some mulled wine and they were seated beside the river, toasting nicely in the warmth of a patio heater, she turned the conversation round to people they knew and old school memories. This was far safer ground than the fact that he'd turned into the sort of guy you looked at twice (and then glanced at again, to make sure your eyes hadn't being playing tricks on you).

"So what took you to Australia?" she asked. "That seems like quite a step for a Cornish boy."

"Yeah, it was a bit further than crossing the Tamar," Rob agreed. He swirled his drink thoughtfully. "I think I just needed to get away from being here and always being the same guy. I was pretty shy at school, and when my uncle offered to have me come out to work for him it seemed too good an opportunity to turn down."

"So you stayed for fourteen years?" Gemma said, a bit enviously. It made getting as far as London seem a bit lame.

"Yes and no. I travelled too. I did the backpacker thing: Thailand, the Far East, all the usual stuff. Then I had a surfy phase and lived in Sydney for a while." His eyes twinkled in the flickering light from the hurricane lamp on their table. "It was brilliant, you know, and I loved every minute. It did me the world of good too. The Aussies I met in the outback were a hard-working bunch, and I had to toughen up pretty quickly if I was going to survive. It felt as though everything out there pretty much wanted to kill me or eat me. Including the women!"

Several of the women in The Schooner looked as though they'd like to eat Rob alive too, Gemma thought with a smile. There were quite a few envious looks being thrown her way; that was for sure! She sucked in her stomach – her old black dress was stretchy, thank goodness – and tucked her hair behind her ears. There. She could still just about pull it off, even if the dress was a tad tight. That was Cal's fault: she'd been comfort eating ever since his earlier phone call.

What was Cal doing now? It was early evening, so maybe he was just finishing up in the bakery? Or perhaps he was having drinks in the Hall with Lady D? Or maybe, and this felt as though somebody was dragging barbed wire through her insides, he was exchanging tender Christmas kisses with Aoife?

This thought made Gemma feel very angry indeed. How dare he? Well, two could play at that game.

"Where did you go after Sydney and the Far East?" she asked Rob, leaning forward a little to give him a good view of her cleavage. Actually, this didn't take much effort; recently her boobs seemed to have been taking on a life of their own. The hopeless washing machine at the Lion Lodge kept shrinking all her bras.

"Then I went to New Zealand," Rob continued. Full marks that his eyes hadn't drifted south, Gemma thought. Ripping her thoughts back to the present she tuned into what he was telling her about life amongst the Kiwis. He had a way of talking to you that made you feel as though you were the most fascinating person on the planet – not like Cal, who was constantly taking calls, speaking to the crew or signing autographs. Cal was great fun and wherever he went he was generally the centre of attention, which sometimes made Gemma feel a bit like a member of his entourage rather than the woman he loved.

Or rather, the woman he used to love.

"So that was where I had my tattoo done," Rob was saying with a rueful grin. "It seemed like a great idea at the time – I guess I was doing the whole Maori thing – but my mum flipped when she saw it."

"It can't be that bad, surely?" Gemma said. Cal had "Made in Ireland" and the Irish flag inked on his bum, which always made her laugh, and the Dangers' emblem was on his back. Still, he wasn't quite at Beckham's level of tattoos yet – although he was always on about getting her name written on his arm. She should have taken him up on it, Gemma thought wryly; maybe he could have had "Gemma's" inked on his willy?

In answer to her question, Rob stood up and slowly began to unbutton his shirt. Gemma gulped and heads swivelled because it was like watching a virtual reality female fantasy. In a minute he'd crook his finger and half the women in the pub would get up and follow him!

Shirt undone, Rob shrugged it from his shoulders and suddenly Gemma realised what he was doing. The midnight-black tattoo was a Maori design and covered most of the right side of his chest, coiling over his shoulder and winding its way down that strong arm. It was tribal, tracing the sinews and the strength beneath the golden skin, and very, very sexy. Gemma's mouth was dry. Cal's flag seemed a bit half-hearted now.

"Oh!" she said. "Did it hurt?"

Did it hurt? What on earth was the matter with her? A gorgeous man had just stripped off and shown her his amazing body and all she could think of to say was *did it hurt?* Cal had said that "Made in Ireland" had caused him to faint, but then he was a footballer and everybody knew they were total pussies when it came to pain.

But Rob just laughed. "Yeah, it hurt like hell! I would have cried like a baby, only the guy doing it would have never let me forget." He pulled the shirt back on and there was a collective sigh of disappointment from the nearby women. "So that's me and the potted history of my last decade or so."

This was where Gemma was supposed to reciprocate with tales of what she'd been up to, but all that was all pretty well documented. As she sipped her drink, not really enjoying it that much, she told Rob a bit about the business and the show.

"I must confess I have seen it," he said, looking shyly at her from under those thick lashes (totally wasted on a guy). "Oh look, who am I kidding? I've seen all of the last series on Netflix."

"You're out of date then. I'll have to get Seaside Rock to send you a disc of the latest one," Gemma said, but Rob shook his head and then reached out and took her hand in his. It was large and work roughened and looked odd when she was so used to seeing Cal's hand with its pastry-crusted nails and speckling of cinnamon freckles.

"I was only watching it because of you," Rob said softly. The lamplight softened his face as he reached across and with his other hand gently traced the curve of her cheek. "I even came to the book signing in Truro the other week. You didn't recognise me and it was so busy I never had time to introduce myself."

She stared at him. Was Rob the fit guy Angel had been struck by? Duh. Of course he was.

"You came to my signing? Why would you do that?"

He smiled bashfully. "Because I couldn't resist seeing you again. Gemma, I had the biggest crush on you at school. You must have realised?"

"You hardly spoke to me in five years!"

"I was tongue-tied every time I looked at you," Rob confessed. "I'm blushing now and I'm thirty. Gemma, I used to have all these conversations planned out in my head and then the minute I saw you they'd all just evaporate. Totally pathetic, I know, but I idolised you."

Now it was Gemma's turn to be tongue-tied. She'd had no idea of any of this.

"Do you remember the Year-Eleven Prom?" Rob asked.

Gemma nodded. She'd lived on Slimfast for days beforehand so that she could squeeze the zip up on her dress; she'd actually become quite addicted to the strawberry flavour. She'd been violently sick after drinking too many alcopops on an empty stomach, and somewhere along the line she'd snogged Brett James, whose dad ran the local garage. Brett had been a dreadful kisser, like a washing machine on spin cycle, but then again she probably hadn't been too great herself after all the throwing up. Poor old Brett. Had Rob even been there?

"I spent weeks plucking up the courage to ask you out," he said quietly. "But I bottled that as usual. I was going to ask you to dance but then I saw you kissing that guy from the garage – he runs it now, by the way, and he's got about five kids – so I went home."

Gemma stared at him, horrified.

"That was when I decided that I wasn't going back to sixth form," he said, finishing his drink and smiling at her. "I didn't want to be that pathetic loser any more. I wanted to be a new person and have a fresh start. As it turned out, that was the best decision I could have made because it led to my travels and all the things that happened afterwards."

"Rob, I am so sorry," Gemma said, squeezing his fingers. "I can honestly say I had no idea you felt like that."

He squeezed back and then let her hand go. "Of course you didn't! How could you when I didn't speak? Anyway, that was a long time ago. I was just trying to explain why I was so peculiar when we were kids. I'm better now, I promise."

He certainly was. Gemma couldn't remember what she'd ever seen in Brett James. Mentally kicking her sixteen-year-old self for her bad taste in men, she let Rob gently steer the conversation back to safer waters:

people they knew in common, and less awkward memories of school. By the time her brothers joined them – both pretty merry, and Kev rocking a tinsel halo and bauble earrings – the tense atmosphere of earlier had vanished and everyone was truly in the Christmas spirit. Even Kirsty didn't seem half as annoying after a few sips of mulled wine.

"Just the one, sis?" Dave raised an eyebrow when he noticed that she was still nursing the same glass Rob had bought her at the start of the evening. "What a lightweight."

Gemma was a bit surprised herself; normally she could drink mulled wine as though it was Ribena. This evening, however, she just wasn't enjoying the taste. It was a bit metallic and weird. She guessed that after everything that had happened with Cal she wasn't really in the mood to celebrate.

Rob glanced at his watch and pulled a face. "Sorry to be a party pooper, folks, but the cows don't know it's Christmas and I've got an early start in the morning."

It was almost last orders anyway, even though the locals were bound to stay for a lock-in. Gemma didn't expect to see her brothers back before Santa had been.

"I'll come too," she said, stifling a yawn. Goodness, she was so tired. "I'm nearly thirty now and I need my beauty sleep."

"Never," Rob said softly. There was a look in his emerald eyes that made the breath catch in Gemma's throat. He picked up her coat and helped her on with it – which made a change from Cal watching her get in a knot – and together they walked through the pub and out into the darkness. The lights were on in the church on the other side of the river, and the strains of "Once in Royal David's City" drifted on the breeze while the stars shone as brightly above the valley as they had in Bethlehem on that very first Christmas Eve. It was Midnight Mass and everyone from Kenniston would be going to the chapel to sing carols and hear the nine lessons. Gemma loved the tiny chapel with its old pews worn smooth by years of being sat on by Elliott bottoms – and Midnight Mass, always the official start of her birthday, was one of her favourite events of the year.

Last year she and Cal had risen at first light to go to Kenniston and get stuck into cooking the Christmas dinner. Cal had mixed Buck's Fizz for her birthday and hidden a beautiful Swarovski heart pendant in a mince pie. Gemma had nearly broken a tooth finding it, but the pain had been worthwhile because it had been such a wonderful thing for him to do. Cal had a romantic streak a mile wide and loved planning surprises and grand gestures, from midnight picnics to treasure hunts. Or rather, he used to love doing these things. Gemma couldn't remember the last time Cal had done something romantic. Sharing the hot-water bottle was about it recently. Realising how much things had changed made her feel desperately sad. Perhaps the lack of sweet notes and romance was the biggest indication of all that he didn't want her anymore.

Gemma wondered what Cal was doing now. Was he at church? Would he have a drink up at the big house before walking home and going to bed? And was Cal going to bed alone? Or was Aoife keeping him company?

Arrah! She had to stop thinking like this! It was going to drive her crazy.

As Rob drove back to the farm in his sexy black Discovery, all tinted windows and black leather seats, Gemma tried to ignore the churning misery in her stomach and focused on chatting as though she hadn't a care in the world. This wasn't hard at all because Rob was very easy to talk to and great company. As he pulled up outside the farm he was telling her such a sweet story about how he'd warmed a little lamb up on the heated leather seat; Gemma managed to make the right responses, despite her mind being elsewhere.

Just stop thinking about Cal, she told herself furiously. There was a seriously gorgeous man here who'd had a childhood crush on her and was a perfect gentleman. He even had a sprig of mistletoe in his hand, which he was laughingly telling her he'd pinched from the big bunch in the pub.

"You never know when it may come in handy," he said with a smile, and those green eyes danced. "We lonely farmers have to make our own luck!"

This was it. Fate herself couldn't have made it any more obvious if she'd been yelling "Snog him!" with a megaphone.

"Same for farmers' daughters," Gemma replied. "Happy Christmas, Rob."

Before she could chicken out, she reached across and brushed her lips against his. His mouth was warm and everything a man's should be. There was a little quiver in the pit of her stomach, which felt very much like desire. Encouraged by this, she was about to lean across for another kiss when Rob ducked his head and kissed her softly on the cheek instead.

"Gemma, it's not me you want," he said gently. "It wasn't when we were sixteen and it isn't now."

She stared at him, mortified. "Rob, I–"

Rob brushed a curl away from her face. "It's not that I don't want to – God knows, I've been thinking of nothing else all evening – but I'm not a fool, Gemma. I know when a woman is in love with somebody else. You love Cal. It's as plain as day. He's the one you want to be with."

It had to be one of the greatest ironies of all time, thought Gemma, that here she was with one of the most beautiful men on the planet – a man who ticked all of her boxes and had told her that he'd been crazy about her for years – and he was turning her down because she was still in love with Cal. The same Cal who was probably with his gorgeous ex-girlfriend at this very minute, not sparing Gemma a second thought.

She stared at Rob and then exhaled slowly because he was right, wasn't he? She did love Cal and he was the one she wanted. He didn't have Rob's film-star looks or amazing body – but none of that mattered, because he was just Cal. She loved his crazy curly hair, daft sense of humour, bad taste in sports gear and squidgy tummy. She loved *him*. She totally and utterly loved Callum South.

What a bloody mess. It was like arriving at Cadbury World and realising you'd gone off chocolate!

"But it's over with Cal," she whispered, and the pain of hearing it aloud was indescribable. What on earth was she doing here? She should have been with Cal for Christmas, working through everything and trying to sort things out. What they had was wonderful and worth fighting for. She must have been mad to step back and let Aoife have him.

"I've missed my chance, I know that," said Rob quietly, "but there's still a chance for you and Cal if you really want to take it. I can see how you feel about him. Besides, don't you think the guy deserves to know that he's going to be a dad?"

"What?" There was a buzzing in Gemma's ears and the car seemed to be spinning around. "What? What did you just say?"

Rob looked puzzled. "I'm a bloke, but not an idiot. You're distracted, you're not drinking and you look exhausted. You're pregnant, aren't you? Come on, Gemma. I've seen enough pregnant cows in my time to know. Not that you're anything like a cow!" he added hastily.

Gemma was suddenly far too busy doing some basic maths to be insulted by this comparison. Rob might not be an idiot but she certainly was.

Oh. My. God.

Now it was all starting to fall into place. The pitiless sense of exhaustion, being emotional, feeling nauseous, her boobs trying to compete with Fifi's, the ever-tightening waistbands even though she'd had a phase of eating less...

"You didn't know, did you?" asked Rob. He looked stricken. "Oh Gemma, I'm sorry; I thought you must know and be afraid to say."

Gemma shook her head. "I didn't... I don't..."

Her brain was racing. She'd been so caught up with the whole Aoife business that she'd not really paid attention to much at all, even something as obvious as her own body. So much suddenly made sense. Of course. Of course...

Gemma's hands were shaking. All she wanted to do was call Cal and tell him, but instinct told her that this was the last thing she should do. Cal had to want to be with her because he loved Gemma the way that she loved him – the love so much a part of yourself that it was in your every cell and every heartbeat, the other person the first thought when you woke up and the last when you fell asleep. Spending the rest of her life wondering whether he was only with her out of obligation would be like the slowest and most painful death imaginable.

"It's Christmas Day," Rob said, pointing to the clock on the dashboard. He kissed her cheek; this time it was a chaste kiss, unplugged from the crackling electricity of earlier. "Happy Christmas birthday, Gemma. I really hope you manage to work it out with Cal."

"Happy Christmas, Rob," Gemma said, kissing him back. Not a frisson or a jolt of anything now. She couldn't help being relieved. "I hope so too, but somehow I doubt it."

And Happy Christmas to you too, Cal, she added silently, once Rob had driven away and she was alone under the starry sky. *I think you're going to be very surprised when you find out what Santa's brought us this year!*

Chapter 20

If this was what being thirty felt like then Gemma wished she'd stuck at twenty-nine. Every bone in her body ached, her breakfast was curdling in her stomach and the smell of the cooking Christmas dinner threatened to send her retching to the bathroom. She was retching and wretched, Gemma thought miserably, as she sat curled up on the sofa with the *Bread and Butlers* Christmas special playing in the background and a glass of untouched Buck's Fizz in her hand. So far she'd managed to avoid sherry, mulled wine and even the Baileys, but Gemma knew it was only because her mother was so busy cooking and her brothers were out working on the farm that nobody had time to think this suspiciously out of character.

How on earth had she managed to miss the fact that she was pregnant? Gemma couldn't believe she'd been so swept up in all the drama that she'd failed to notice something so fundamental. In fairness to her, she had always been irregular – crash diets and stress not helping matters much – and her love life had been fairly sparse lately. But even so...

As soon as Rob's comment had left his very kissable lips (she couldn't really think like this anymore, could she?), everything had fallen into place like counters slotting into the winning line in a game of Connect Four. All the anomalies of the past few months, the bone-grinding exhaustion, the ridiculously over-the-top emotions, the lurking nausea and even the tightening of her waistbands – although in fairness this wasn't really anything unusual – made perfect sense. Gemma didn't need to drive to a late-night chemist and demand a test to know that Rob was right: every fibre of her being told her he was spot on. Still, this morning she'd gone online to find the nearest emergency chemist and driven over to pick up a test. Peeing on a stick in a public loo wasn't quite the setting Gemma had imagined for the discovery of her first pregnancy, but there'd been no way she could wait a second longer. She'd done the deed and then sat on the loo seat, her heart racing while the longest three minutes in history passed. Sure enough two blue lines had duly appeared.

So. There it was. The undeniable truth. She was up the duff. Knocked up. Had a baker's bun in the oven. It didn't matter how you described it; the question was, what on earth was she going to do? Things between her and Cal could scarcely be worse. How could she break this news to him now?

As she watched the on-screen Angel and Laurence greeting their guests, Gemma chewed her nails and tried to think of a solution. When Cal appeared, looking gorgeous in a moss-green cord shirt and faded Levi's, her heart felt as though it was going to punch its way through her ribcage. What was she doing here, so far away from him? It wasn't long ago that they'd told one another everything, even waking up in the night to talk things over or share ideas for new recipes and ventures. When did things change?

Around the time that Cal began visiting his ex-girlfriend in London and lying about it, that's when, Gemma thought sadly. She guessed that if he wanted to be with Aoife then that was something she would just have to come to terms with, no matter how much it hurt. Although she was desperate to call Cal and tell him her news, Gemma knew that she couldn't breathe a word until she'd established exactly what was going on. If Cal wanted to be with Aoife then Gemma needed to know this for certain; she had to hear it from him, otherwise how would she ever be sure that he was with her for the right reasons rather than out of some misplaced sense of duty? Gemma couldn't think of anything more painful than spending the rest of her life wondering whether Cal was only with her because he was doing the right thing while deep down wishing he could have been with another woman.

No. There was no way she could speak to Cal about this until she knew what was really happening with him and Aoife. For now she was on her own.

Gemma's hand fluttered to her stomach and rested there wonderingly. Everything felt just the same as it always had – and yet all of her instincts told her without a shred of doubt that it was all totally and utterly different. So maybe she wasn't entirely on her own? Not if she really was going to have a baby! Her stomach lurched with sudden terror. Oh Lord. Was she fully ready for this? Was anyone ever ready?

On the screen the guests were arriving at Kenniston and gathering in the Great Hall by the Christmas tree, sipping champagne and kissing hello. The camera was following Fifi's entrance now. She was poured into a bodycon dress that wouldn't have conned anyone, given that her famous assets were well and truly displayed in all their fake-tanned and glitter-dusted glory – and she was flinging her arms around Cal. Even though Gemma knew that there was nothing between Fifi and Cal, and that she'd only been invited because she was TV gold, seeing a glamour model all over the man she loved was more than Gemma could stand. Picking up the remote control, she turned the television off with a howl of misery.

"Are you all right, love?" Demelza Pengelley appeared in the doorway, apron on and face flushed from the heat of the kitchen. She glanced across at the television and frowned. "Aren't you going to watch Cal on the show?"

Gemma shook her head. She couldn't do it.

"But it's the live Christmas special!" Wiping her hands on her apron, Gemma's mother joined her on the sofa. "Don't you want to see what they're all up to? And Cal too, of course."

The room blurred as Gemma's eyes swam with tears. She couldn't bear to watch Cal having fun at Kenniston without her, to know that he'd chosen Aoife and the show over her, to wish with all her heart that things had worked out differently...

"Sweetheart, these are your friends and this live show is a really big deal for them," Demelza insisted, reaching for the remote control. "I really think you ought to watch."

What on earth had got into her mother, thought Gemma, feeling rather irritated. Normally Demelza was oblivious to the television, and she'd never shown any great interest in *Bread and Butlers* before. The Pengelleys were generally far too busy with the farm to watch reality TV. How her mother knew that today was a live show was a total mystery.

"Mum! You do know that Cal and I have broken up? It's over with us!" Gemma flared. Once spoken the words sounded harsh and ugly, hanging in the air like the trails of sparklers on Bonfire Night, real now and horribly final. She gulped back her misery and added, "He's with his ex-girlfriend now, and if you don't mind I'd rather not watch it all being played out on national television."

Her mother's eyes widened. "I knew you two were having problems but I had no idea you'd split up forever. And Cal's with his ex-girlfriend? When did all this happen?"

Gemma shrugged. "About the same time he refused to tell me why he's been secretly meeting his ex in London?"

"Oh Gemma," sighed her mother, "not this still? Why can't you just trust him when he says it's innocent? He's said he'll explain. Why won't you wait until he does that before making any decisions in anger?"

"You're taking his side?" Gemma was outraged. Weren't your parents supposed to root for you? Her hand fluttered to her stomach. She'd defend this little person to the death. There was no way she'd stick up for its cheating, fibbing partner.

"Gemma, this isn't about sides: it's about give and take and trusting your partner," Demelza told her wearily. "Relationships are never black and white, love. They're messy and they're blooming hard work. There's a reason why fairy tales end with a wedding – that's the part where the graft really starts." She rose from the sofa and handed the remote control back to her daughter. "Before you offer, I don't need any help in the kitchen. Just watch the show. You never know, it might help."

Personally Gemma though watching *Bread and Butlers*, a show that she partially held responsible for the crumbling of her relationship with Cal, would be about as much use as boiling water in a chocolate kettle. Besides, she had no intention of torturing herself further by watching Cal's antics. Instead she flipped to an ancient Bond movie and pretended to be glued to Roger Moore as he raced speedboats, seduced women with big hair and raised his eyebrow at villains. By the time Bond had saved the world, the *Bread and Butlers* Christmas special was long finished.

This was torture. Cal was the only person Gemma wanted to speak to – the only person she could talk to about the shock of suddenly realising she was pregnant – and he'd never been further away from her. She was thirty, pregnant and all alone; this wasn't how she'd pictured Christmas when she'd booked the cottage for her and Cal, Gemma reflected sadly. Some thirtieth birthday this had turned out to be. It was always rubbish having your birthday on Christmas Day, but this was something again.

Christmas dinner passed in a blur for Gemma. As always the food was wonderful because Demelza Pengelley was a fantastic cook, but for once Gemma's appetite had vanished. It didn't matter that the roast potatoes were crispy and golden with goose fat and fluffy inside, or that the turkey was moist, the gravy was as rich as Croesus and the chestnut stuffing melted in the mouth; her throat was too tight with misery to swallow even the smallest mouthful. Great. Not only had Cal ruined her birthday and broken her heart, but now he'd even stopped her from enjoying her Christmas dinner. While Gemma's brothers heaped their plates several times over, she picked at her food and felt alarmed that all of a sudden the sprouts seemed appealing. When she found herself about to spoon a third helping onto her plate, Gemma caught herself just in the nick of time. If passing on the wine hadn't already made her sharp-eyed mother suspicious, then seeing her daughter tucking into sprouts really would raise the red flag. Gemma was still trying to get her own head around what was happening to her; the last thing she needed right now was her mother on the case.

Once pudding was eaten, the dishwasher was thrumming away in the kitchen and the family was hunkered down in front of the fire with a tin of Quality Street and the *EastEnders* special, Gemma decided it was time to get some fresh air. Pulling on her boots and the old waxed jacket, she set off across the fields.

It was a bright but cold afternoon and already the sun looked like a red Babybel balancing on the horizon. The cows huddled against the hedges and Gemma's boots crunched over the still-frozen ridges of plough. Rather than climbing the hill as she had yesterday (Yesterday? How was it possible that so much had changed in twenty-four hours?), Gemma turned away from the farm and headed into the woods, where the only noises were the rooks caw-cawing and the snapping of twigs underfoot. Dapples of late afternoon sunshine danced through the branches, while above them seagulls wheeled high in the cloudless sky. Almost without realising what she was doing, Gemma found herself choosing the lower path that zigzagged through the trees and down to Penmerryn Creek.

Talk about wanting to torture yourself, Gemma thought grimly. She dug her hands into her pockets; outside the shelter of the woods there was a chilly wind whipping up the river, numbing her fingers and slicing into her cheeks. Yes, what great idea this was! Why not revisit the place where she and Cal had been so happy and rub it in a little more?

She paused at the water's edge and glanced across at the cottage. The renovations were finished now, by the looks of it. The windows were sparkling and the woodwork was freshly painted in a minty green. Even the garden had been tidied up, and a small Christmas tree had been placed outside the front door. The new owners must have arrived for their first Christmas in their Cornish bolthole. Maybe even now they were in front of the wood burner and toasting their good luck? The car was pulled up on the freshly raked gravel. It was the same sporty black BMW that belonged to the scary woman with the bob. Next to it was a white Range Rover just like the one Cal owned.

Wait a minute...

Gemma's eyes narrowed. Maybe it was a hitting-thirty thing and her eyesight was on the blink, but for a moment she could have sworn that *was* Cal's Range Rover. The model was exactly the same and it even had an identical dent in the right wing where somebody *might* have accidentally clouted it on the Lion Lodge's gatepost. (Not that that particular somebody had been Gemma. Of course not. How that dent had got there remained a complete and utter mystery!)

Shading her eyes against the brightness of the setting sun, Gemma walked a little closer to the cottage until she could see quite clearly the registration plate of the car. This was when her heart really did begin to hammer like rain on a barn roof. There was absolutely no mistaking that personalised registration, picked out in tasteful gold and, as Cal had teasingly assured her, every bit as much a vital part of the Premier League footballer's kit as the WAGs and mock-Tudor mansions.

It was, without a shadow of a doubt, Cal's car.

Gemma's head was spinning. It wasn't possible. Cal was in Devon. He'd been in a live TV show only a few hours earlier, so there was no way he could be in Cornwall already – and even if he were in Cornwall, why on earth would he be down at Penmerryn Creek? It just didn't make any sense.

Mysteries were not Gemma's forte. She never watched *Sherlock* or *Midsomer Murders* because trying to figure out the answers always gave her a mammoth headache. Unlike Angel, who thrived on complications, Gemma much preferred life to be straightforward. That was one of the things she'd always loved so much about Cal: he didn't have a tricky or deceitful bone in his body. He was honest and kind and a completely open book.

Or so she'd thought. How ironic that, as it turned out, Gemma didn't actually know the man she loved at all…

She picked up pace – all that tramping up and down the drive to Kenniston had made her fitter than she'd realised – and stomped along the path to the cottage. Her heart pounding painfully, Gemma took a deep breath and then banged her fist on the door. Whatever Cal was up to, whatever games he was playing, it was time he told the truth. Whatever it was and however much it hurt her, she had to know.

"Just coming!" called a cheerful female voice, followed by the sounds of footsteps on flagstones. "One minute!"

Gemma felt the blood freeze in her veins, and for a horrible minute she thought she was going to pass out. There was absolutely no mistaking those lilting Irish tones – no mistaking them at all.

Aoife O'Shaughnessy was here with Cal.

Chapter 21

"Oh my God! Gemma!"

If circumstances had been different, i.e. if she hadn't just discovered beyond all reasonable doubt that the man she loved really was seeing his ex-girlfriend, Gemma would have found Aoife's expression of total horror comical. Whoever it was that the Irish woman had expected to see on the doorstep, it certainly wasn't Gemma; Aoife's green eyes were wide with shock. As usual she looked Photoshop perfect with her glossy dark hair, peachy skin and slim figure, but for once Gemma was beyond caring. It didn't matter that her own nose was red with cold and her hair whipped into a bird's nest by the wind, or that she was wearing a rather stinky wax jacket that she suspected the dogs had been sleeping on. All she wanted was to find Cal.

"Yes, it's 'Oh My God Gemma'," she agreed calmly, amazed that her voice sounded low and reasonable when she was teetering on the brink of doing the full fishwife. "I've come to see Cal, Aoife, and this time please don't lie to me and pretend you haven't seen him for months. We both know he's here."

Aoife gulped. "He is here, Gemma, but it's not what you think."

"Oh please!" Gemma raised her eyes to the heavens. "It's exactly what I think. Let's not waste any more time. Where is he?" She glanced over Aoife's slender shoulder and peered into the hallway. Goodness, for a renovated house this place looked pretty unfinished. The walls were smoothly plastered in pink, yet remained unpainted; the light fittings were just bare wires protruding from the walls; and the skirting boards were still plain wood. There was no smell of Christmas dinner either, which was odd. Cal loved Christmas dinner, and he would have missed the one at Kenniston. Why would he and Aoife run away to an unfinished cottage? Was Gemma going mad?

Her head swimming, Gemma clutched at the doorframe. The world cartwheeled around her and black dots speckled her vision. Moments later she was slumped in the hall with her back against the bare plastered wall and her head between her knees while the place went round and round like something from Disneyland. *It's a Small World* would be appropriate, Gemma thought bleakly. Why, Cal! Fancy bumping into you and your lover in the very place where we promised we'd be together forever. What a big surprise.

God, she hated surprises. In Gemma's experience they never turned out well.

A glass of water was pressed into her hand. Cal was crouching next to her and stroking her cheek tenderly. His usually happy face was filled with concern and his brow furrowed.

"Drink this," he said gently, helping her raise the glass to her lips. "Little sips, now. That's grand. You're doing grand, so you are."

Gemma sipped, although what she really wanted to do was drown Cal in the tumbler of water. How dare he look so worried and so normal? He was putting his arm around her now as though everything was fine and she hadn't just discovered him shacked up in his love nest with his ex-girlfriend. Cal looked so utterly like his usual self, with his curls standing at odd angles and his sleepy eyes crinkling at her as he smiled, that it all seemed impossible; yet here she was, in the cottage they'd dreamed about and with Aoife hovering nervously like an anxious butterfly.

"Don't touch me," she muttered to Cal, shaking him off. "How could you do this to me? I gave you so many chances to tell the truth about you and her, and you still lied through your teeth." Her eyes filled and Gemma blinked the tears away furiously. There was no way she'd give the pair of them the satisfaction of seeing her cry. Sitting on the floor like this, all of her dignity was gone. She smelt of old dog and felt as though she was close to throwing up. But Gemma wasn't going to dissolve into tears. Not until she'd ripped Cal's head off and beaten him with the soggy end, anyway.

Cal sighed. "Ah, Gemma, I know this looks bad and, yes, I haven't told you the truth."

"'Looks bad'?" Gemma couldn't help laughing at this. Cal was always one for an understatement. Like when he'd told her he had *quite* a big tax bill or that Mammy South was visiting just for a *few* days, which had actually turned out to be three weeks. "Cal, I've caught you here with Aoife, who you denied over and over again you ever see. I don't think it gets any worse!"

For a moment Cal looked as though he was going to try to deny it yet again. Then he shrugged and gave her a rueful smile. "You're right, darlin': I have been keeping a big secret from you. I know how it all looks and, believe me, there've been so many times when I've just wanted to tell you the truth."

So it was true. Gemma hadn't realised just how much she'd been longing to hear Cal say that she was mistaken. Even with her scarf wrapped around her throat and wearing the thick wax jacket, she felt icy cold. It was over. Cal really was in love with Aoife.

"Gemma, listen to me, so." Taking the glass away, Cal took her cold hands in his. "The secret I've been keeping, it really isn't what you think. Yes, Aoife is involved, but very indirectly, and I swear on my mammy's life only in a professional legal capacity."

She stared at him. "I don't understand."

Cal tightened his grasp on her hands and his big brown eyes twinkled down into hers. "Gemma, I bought the cottage! I only bloody managed to buy it! I knew how much it meant to you and," he winked, "after that afternoon we spent here I was pretty fond of the auld place myself. So, I managed to do some digging and with the help of your mammy and daddy I persuaded the owners to sell it."

Gemma felt as though she'd stepped into some weird parallel universe. "You've bought the cottage for us? And my parents know about it?"

Cal nodded, his curls bouncing merrily. "Sure, and hasn't it cost me an arm and a leg? No wonder I had no money and had to work so bloody hard. But I knew what it meant to you, Gem, and it's time we had a place of our own, so. I've been frantically hoping it would be ready for your birthday. The money from the show should hopefully pay for the last bits and pieces." He grinned. "Now do you see why I had to keep going? Anton Yuri would have released me but, sweet Jaysus, I needed the money! This place gobbles it!"

It was too much to take in. Cal had bought and renovated the cottage for her? And as a birthday present? Gemma wanted to pinch herself; this had to be a dream.

"But what about Aoife?" she asked. "You were seeing her in London, weren't you?"

"Sure," admitted Cal, smiling at Aoife, who was still looking worried. "I couldn't have done any of this without her. She's my project manager. This is what she does. Aoife and her partner Lucy develop and manage investment portfolios. I couldn't tell you the truth because I didn't want to spoil the surprise. Saying that, all but splitting up with you because it looked so bad on my part kind of took the edge off a little. You should have trusted me, Gem. I love you and I swear I'd never cheat."

Gemma felt terrible. She'd been so quick to judge – although, in her defence, the evidence had seemed pretty damning.

"Cal's been working with me and my partner, Lucy," Aoife said softly, stepping forward and fixing Gemma with her clear green-eyed gaze. "'Partner' as in my girlfriend, as well as my business associate. You really don't have anything to worry about, Gemma. I promise. You never did. I'm more likely to fancy you than Cal!"

It was just as well that Gemma was already sitting down, because this was a bombshell she really hadn't been expecting. Scary black-bob lady, she who shouted at people trying to peek into cottages, was Aoife's girlfriend? Aoife, whom she'd been so certain was out to steal Cal away, wasn't even interested in men? Seriously?

"But you dated Cal," Gemma said, totally thrown, and Aoife laughed.

"Yes, for about ten minutes when I was fourteen and before I acknowledged that I really wasn't into guys. I think Cal knew the truth about me long before I reached that point."

"Sure, if you didn't fancy me you had to be gay, so," teased Cal, and Aoife rolled her eyes at him.

"Men, you're all the same. Jaysus, you'll be offering to convert me in a minute," she complained.

Gemma stared at her, fascinated, watching the ice maiden melt before her eyes. Or maybe Aoife had never been an ice maiden in the first place and it was only her own insecurities that had convinced Gemma otherwise? The truth had been there all the time.

"Why didn't you tell me?" she asked Cal. "Why the big secret?"

"My mother is very old fashioned," Aoife said before Cal could reply. "She's just like Cal's mammy in that respect. When she finds out, then it should be me she hears it from. I owe her that much."

Gemma thought of Mammy South. *Old fashioned* was putting it politely.

"Cal was the first person I told the truth about me," Aoife continued. "He's kept my secret for years and I trust him totally. In London it's simple. Lucy and I have our private life away from home, but my mother would be so shocked if she ever found out. I'm going to tell her very soon because Lucy and I want to get married, but the news has to come from me and I have to tell her in my way. It can't come from anyone else."

"That's why I couldn't tell you there was absolutely nothing to worry about, no matter how much I longed to," Call said tenderly. He knitted his fingers with Gemma's and dropped a kiss onto her knuckles. "It wasn't my secret to tell."

Gemma's heart melted because this was Cal all over. It would have made his life a thousand times easier if he had just told her the truth about Aoife – but he'd never betray a confidence, just as he'd never break the contract with Seaside Rock and let the team down. It was what had made him such a brilliant captain for the Dangers and why she should have known better than to ever doubt him. When Cal gave his word it was rock solid.

"Lucy and I are in Cornwall for Christmas because we were planning to help Cal finish the last bits on the cottage," Aoife was saying, just in case there was still any doubt. "Gemma, Cal's employing me and he's the most loyal person on earth. He's never breathed a word about my personal life, even to you. I promise he would never, ever betray you."

She shook her head. "I don't know about you guys, but I've had more than enough of secrets. Total honesty: that's going to be my New Year's resolution. And if you guys will excuse me, I'm going to get back to Talland Bay where there's a hotel, a Christmas dinner and somebody very special waiting for me."

The front door clicked shut behind Aoife, and she was gone. Moments later her car crunched over the drive and Cal and Gemma were alone in the cottage. It smelled of new wood and paint and possibilities. Cal raised Gemma to her feet and pulled her close. Instantly she felt all the tension and despair of the past few weeks slip away. He fitted perfectly in her arms, and he felt so right.

"I love you, Cal," Gemma whispered into his chest. "I'm so sorry I didn't trust you."

As she looked up at him again, Cal's hands cupped her face and he gently brushed the tears from her cheeks. Then he bent his head and kissed her. It was just the softest of kisses, but one that made her shiver all over – and with desire this time, rather than from the cold.

"You planned all of this for me," she said, still unable to quite believe this. It was hardly surprising that her friends and family hadn't seemed to back her. "Everyone knew, didn't they? Angel? My folks?"

Cal pulled a face. "Angel could get blood from a stone, so she could. I couldn't keep it from her; she was ready to kill me for cheating on you, so she was, and I feared for my life. She went mad that Laurence already knew."

"Laurence knew about this too?"

He nodded. "Laurence has been grand. If anyone knows how hard it is to rebuild a house, it's him! Sure, he gave me as much extra film work as he could find but, Jaysus, I thought it would kill me at times on top of the bakery. Laurence always knew that I was going to escape for Christmas to be with you here. The original plan was that I'd tell you after the Christmas show – that was my last one – and we'd drive down here together. When it all started to fall apart he told me to go anyway, and feck the contract."

He drew Gemma close and she rested her head against his chest once more.

"You did all this for me and you didn't complain even when I was angry with you?" she said, feeling ashamed. She could feel his heart beating against her cheek – his loving and generous heart. "The cottage was our dream."

When she raised her head, Cal leaned down and rubbed his nose against hers in an Eskimo kiss. "It *is* our dream, you mean. I hope you're ready for it? We are going to escape for Christmas after all! I've left the show now and we'll be moving the business here in the New Year, if that's what you still want?"

He looked so worried as he said this. Gemma tightened her arms around him.

"Of course I want it," she assured him. "I want to be with you more than I've ever wanted anything in my whole life. This cottage, the show, the business even – none of that matters more than being with you."

"Phew," said Cal. "As for the business, I've neglected it something terrible, so I have. It's probably hanging by a bloody thread with those trainees running it. Jaysus, I hope Rick and Jamie still want me to supply their places, otherwise we'll probably starve!" He winked. "I'm teasing, Gem; don't look so worried. Now come on, don't you want to see what's happened to the auld place?"

Gemma certainly did. It had come a long way from the ruins they'd explored before, and hand in hand they wandered through the renovated cottage. Nothing had been decorated yet – because Aoife had been adamant that this was Gemma's job, Cal explained – but it was the perfect blank canvas, and she could see how he'd taken their summer daydreams from that one perfect afternoon and woven them into this special place. It had been done with such love that she could hardly speak. Cal had listened to all her wishes and had quietly gone away and built her dream home. He hadn't expected thanks; he'd worked twice as hard and never complained when she'd been angry with him.

If you needed an example of love then this was it. With love he had made this place – their Christmas escape – their home. And if she was brave enough to tell him her news, maybe it would also be where their future would truly begin?

The final room was the kitchen, which for Gemma and Cal was not just the location for their business and their passion for baking, but the very place where all those months ago they'd held each other closely, gazed up at the summer sky and dreamed. That day when she and Angel had trespassed, Gemma had already seen how the cottage had been extended, and that a glass roof spanned the entire length of the south-facing side. She knew that the sun would pour in during the morning, always the hardest time for an early-rising baker, and stay with them all day as Cal's work finished and Gemma perfected her cakes. It was – as they'd imagined on that summer's day while the wood pigeons had called and the bees had droned among the wildflowers – the perfect spot to house their bakery.

Cal paused on the threshold. He hadn't let go of her hand for a second, but suddenly his fingers were chilly and he was chewing his bottom lip in the way he always did when there was something on his mind. Gemma rose onto her tiptoes and kissed him.

"What is it?" she asked.

"Did you see the show?"

Gemma shook her head. "I turned it off, even though my mother was adamant I should watch it. I only lasted as far as Fifi arriving. I couldn't bear seeing her looking like she was going to jump your bones."

"*My* bones?" laughed Cal. "Sure, you should have stayed tuned! She snogged Dougal under the mistletoe and then they vanished off for ages. Mammy's gone mad, so!"

Gemma grinned at this. Handsome, silver-tongued Dougal was an utter devil, although nothing would convince his mother that he wasn't whiter than the baby Jesus's swaddling bands, and he and Fifi would be a match made in reality-TV heaven. Already Gemma was sure that if Angel had her way there'd soon be another South joining the cast.

"So you never saw what happened next?" Cal continued.

"No." Gemma stepped back and looked up at him. "What?"

He gazed down at her. "I didn't stay. I told them all – and the whole of Britain too, so – that I couldn't be anywhere without you. Then I left. I said I had to be with you, Gemma Pengelley, and then I drove here. There's something I needed to show you."

His brown eyes were bright with emotion. He didn't have to say that he loved her; Gemma knew she would never need to hear it again, because she could see it in his expression.

"The cottage?" she smiled. "That was what you had to show me!"

But Cal didn't speak. Instead, he shook his head and, still holding her hand, led her into the kitchen. Now it was Gemma who couldn't speak, because there simply weren't the words. This was a space that had been created with such love that it took her breath away. Above them, just as they'd envisioned it, was the glass roof. Even on a midwinter's day when the sun had slipped below the hill and the stars were already getting ready for a night out, it flooded the kitchen with light, revealing a flagstone floor and acres of work surfaces. Although the fittings had yet to arrive, Gemma could picture them all perfectly and even smell the bread as it rose in the ovens.

Cal placed his hands on her shoulders and gently turned her to face the far end of the kitchen.

"Happy birthday, happy Christmas, happy Forever," he said softly.

Gemma's hand flew to her mouth – and it was just as well that Cal had her shoulders, because her legs suddenly felt as soft as cookie dough. Positioned exactly where she'd imagined it, and in pride of place, was the cherry-red Aga that she'd dreamed of.

"Open the warming oven." Cal was biting his bottom lip again. "Go on, Gem, have a look."

Still feeling stunned, Gemma did as he suggested, running her hands over the cool shiny enamel in disbelief before unlatching the warming oven. Inside was a box.

"Open it up," Cal urged. He was looking serious now. "Go on, Gem, it's for you."

Intrigued, she lifted the lid. Inside were a key and another box.

"It's the key to the cottage," Cal beamed when she looked at him wonderingly. "Welcome home, Gemma."

Penmerryn Cottage was really her home? It was too much to take in, and with shaking hands she began to unwrap the smaller parcel. Almost before she'd realised what he was doing, Cal was down on one knee in the middle of the kitchen – and Gemma didn't need to finish opening the velvet-lined box to know what was inside.

"I love you, Gemma Pengelley," Cal said quietly. "Sometimes I feck up, I eat too much and I know I have dreadful relatives, but I love you. I never want to be without you again."

The box fell open. Nestled against a bed of shamrock-green velvet was a perfect square solitaire. Gemma's eyes widened.

"Will you marry me?" said Cal. "And give me an answer soon, Gems, because this stone floor is killing me poor auld footballer's knees!"

But Gemma could only nod and smile as Cal rose to his feet and slipped the ring onto her finger. It was a perfect fit, just like he was for her.

"From now on there'll be nothing between us but total trust," Cal promised as he folded her into his arms and brushed his mouth across hers. "Sure, I've learned my lesson, Gem. No matter how good the intentions there'll be nothing but complete trust and honesty between us. I promise. No more secrets."

But as Cal bent to kiss her again, Gemma began to laugh – because there was one very important secret left, wasn't there? A secret that she could hardly wait to share with him, and one that she knew with all her heart was going to make their Christmas escape to Penmerryn Creek absolutely perfect.

"In that case," she said softly, winding her arms around Cal's neck and pulling him closer, until her lips were right against his ear, "there's something very special that I need to tell you…"

THE END

Ruth Saberton is the bestselling author of *Katy Carter Wants a Hero* and *Escape for the Summer*. She also writes upmarket commercial fiction under the pen names Jessica Fox, Georgie Carter and Holly Cavendish.

Born and raised in the UK, Ruth has just returned from living on Grand Cayman for two years. What an adventure!

And since she loves to chat with readers, please do add her as a Facebook friend and follow her on Twitter.

www.ruthsaberton.co.uk

Twitter: @ruthsaberton

Facebook: Ruth Saberton